Finding Forever With You

S.L. STERLING

Chapter One

Sophie

The heat from the morning sun was hot as I made my way down the street to Aroma Mocha. I was on my way to meet Jenna for our usual Saturday morning coffee date." Normally, we walked to Aroma Mocha together after our yoga class, but she couldn't make it this morning. Instead, I made my way to the local cafe and flung my mat under my arm as I pulled the door open and stepped into the amazing smell of roasted coffee beans and freshly baked cinnamon buns. I looked around the dining area for Jenna, and when I didn't see her, I made my way to the counter and placed our usual order, then took a seat in our usual booth. I pulled my cell phone from my yoga bag and quickly checked my messages. I had just finished replying to someone at work when I spotted Jenna entering the small cafe. She spotted me right away and waved as she made her way through the crowd, her cell phone pressed up against her ear.

"I'm sorry, just a second. It's Matt," she mouthed as she pointed to her phone.

I smiled and slid out of my jacket while waiting for my vanilla latte and blueberry muffin to be delivered. I tried not to pay attention to Jenna while she spoke to Matt, but it was impossible. My best friend looked so happy, and I loved how her face lit up as she listened to whatever it was Matt was saying. The excitement in her voice was almost contagious when she responded to him. I wondered what it was like to be as happy as Jenna was. I hadn't had a decent relationship in years—well, honestly, never, but who was counting.

Jenna beamed as she hung up the phone and tucked it into her purse and turned her attention towards me. "Good morning," she sang. "How was yoga?"

"It was yoga. You know, the usual—downward dogs and tree poses. It would have been so much better with you there."

"Yeah, I know. I'm sorry about that. It was a crazy week, and I needed this morning just to lounge around with Matt."

"Yeah, sure, whatever. You know, I recall someone who

so desperately wanted me to join yoga she spouted about how it does a body and mind good to de-stress. Now I go more than her."

"You are right, I did say that, but let's just say that Matt does his best to make sure I stay good and de-stressed." I couldn't help but roll my eyes as she giggled.

"How's Matt?" I questioned, doing my best to change the subject.

"He's good." She got quiet for a moment, a soft smile coming to her lips. "I should probably tell you that I think I might be in love." Jenna swooned. "He is just everything I have ever wanted. I seriously have to ask myself what made me wait so long."

I let out a laugh, leaned across the table, and whispered, "You waited because you were convinced that he was a player."

"I did not. That was what you said."

"You are such a liar! I told you to take the chance."

Jenna laughed as she stirred her coffee with her biscotti. "So tell me, how's everything going with Ralph?" Jenna asked, taking a bite of her coffee-soaked treat.

I looked around the cafe and laughed. "Ha, don't ask. The man is all tongue. I can't even fathom what he'd be like in bed because I can barely get past a kiss."

Jenna began laughing uncontrollably. "Oh God, that reminds me of that guy I dated in university. Do you remember? What was his name?"

"Scott. Who wouldn't remember? But now look who you have," I said, raising my eyebrows suggestively. Jenna had started dating Matt, one of our close friends, not too long ago. I'd always thought that they would be perfect for one another and was so glad that they had finally taken the plunge.

"And look how long it took to find him."

"At least you found him. I'm just stuck with tongue," I murmured, crossing my eyes and sticking out my tongue. We both laughed.

Truth was, I had struggled in every relationship I'd had, the longest lasting just over a year and ending just as I had come off the hardest year of my life. I was convinced now more than ever that I was destined to be alone. I had just celebrated my thirtieth birthday and felt that lately my biological clock was ticking, but without a serious relationship, there wasn't much I could do about it.

"What about one of our circle?" Jenna asked, snapping me back to our conversation.

"What about them?" I questioned.

"Well, you say that ultimately you want a baby, right? You don't sound super keen on staying with Roger, or the Tongue as you call him, so, what about one of our circle? It takes all the risk out of it. I mean, you at least know who the guy is, what he looks like, what he is like."

"And we are going to kill that idea right now."

"What? Why?" Jenna asked innocently.

"Because you are being ridiculous." I shook my head. "The whole idea of that is just not going to happen."

"No, I'm not. What about Brent? I think you two would make a lovely couple. Or Shawn. Oooh, or Dave. He has an eight-pack most girls would kill to touch," she said, raising her eyebrows.

"Oh my God, just stop." I laughed, hiding my face in my hands.

The door to the cafe opened, grabbing Jenna's attention, her eyes lighting up at whatever idea she had now.

"What?" I asked, taking a bite of the still-warm blueberry muffin that I'd been craving all week. Jenna's eyes were still trained on whoever had walked through the door and was at the counter. I turned just in time to see the sexy Chase Malone leaning against the counter ordering his morning coffee, and I looked back towards Jenna, seeing a silly grin on her face.

"Why not?" She shrugged, her eyes lighting up like a Christmas tree.

"Why not what?"

"Why not Chase?"

"Why not Chase what?" I could feel my heart start to beat faster at what I hoped she wasn't trying to suggest.

"O.M.G! Pull your head out of the sand. He is as single as they come, and he is not looking to settle down anytime soon. He's hot, sexy, smart... Borrow some of his best swimmers and be done with it."

I almost spit my coffee all over Jenna at her suggestion. "Oh my God, no!" I said, balling my napkin up and throwing it at her.

"What is wrong with that idea?? What girl on the face of this earth wouldn't want a night, or hell better yet, a few nights with Chase Malone. Seriously, out of all the guys, he'd be your best bet. I've heard he is dynamite in the sack."

I looked up towards the counter and saw Chase give us an innocent wave.

"Seriously, Sophie, come on, just do it."

"Seriously, Jenna, just shut up already! He's my best friend," I gritted out in embarrassment just in time for Chase to slide into the booth beside me.

"Good morning, ladies," he greeted, reaching across the table for the sugar. "What are you beauties up to on this beautiful day?"

"Trying to help Sophie solve her relationship crisis."

"Oh my God, shut up!" I said, burying my face in my hands.

Chase looked at me, smiling. "Oh, Soph, you are too cute. You think you have a relationship problem?"

I looked to Jenna for help, since she was the one who'd started this whole conversation. "Go ahead, Sophie, share with Chase." She grinned.

I shrugged and looked at him. "Perhaps."

"Perhaps, Sophie, it's more of an asshole problem," he

said, winking and pinching my outer arm, trying to lighten the mood just as his cell phone went off.

"What's that supposed to mean?" I questioned.

"It means that you need to find a nice boy." He winked, "Well, ladies, I have to run," he announced, "the world of law is awaiting me. See you ladies next week."

"Absolutely, we wouldn't miss it." Jenna grinned.

I glared at Jenna as she watched Chase leave the cafe. When she finally turned her attention back to me, I didn't know whether to laugh or cry. "Seriously? You think this is funny?"

"Oh come on, lighten up. I'm trying to help."

"Okay, okay," I said, laughing and squirming at the same time. "Perhaps you are right. Maybe I just need to find myself a nice man, but not Chase."

"Okay, not Chase. But I'm not going to sleep until we find you someone!" She giggled, shoving the last piece of biscotti in her mouth.

We sat and talked for a good hour after Chase had left, and finally, after parting ways, I decided to take a walk through the park near my house. I loved walking in early spring, listening to the birds chirp and smelling the crisp air. As I walked, I could still hear Jenna's suggestion at the forefront of my mind. As much as I hated to admit it, she did have a point. I was comfortable with my male friends, and I knew them all well, and perhaps Chase wasn't such a bad choice.

I shook the absurd thought from my head, crossed the street, and entered my apartment building. I took the elevator up to the twentieth floor and opened my door. I dropped my purse on the floor just inside the door and slipped my shoes off. I went into the kitchen and poured myself a glass of orange juice and immediately saw the flashing light on my phone. I dialed into my voicemail while taking a drink of the sweet liquid. The first message was from my boss reminding me of a meeting on Monday morning; the second was Ralph.

I drank down the rest of my orange juice and was just about to call Ralph back when my cell phone vibrated in my pocket. Looking down at the screen, I saw Chase had left me a message.

CHASE: WHAT ABOUT RALPH? HE SEEMS LIKE A STANDUP GUY.

I rolled my eyes. Not him now too. I laughed out loud and texted him back.

ME: HE KISSES LIKE A LIZARD!

I smiled, closed the chat window, and dialed Ralph's number. Within twenty minutes, I had gone from being in a lizard kissing relationship to being very single once again. I threw my phone down on the dining room table and rested my head on my arm. I lay there listening to the silence of my apartment, debating on crying or getting up and carrying on with my life. When my phone vibrated against the tabletop, I grabbed it and saw a message from Chase.

CHASE: EWWW THAT IS GROSS. BET THAT SORT OF MAKES YOU WISH YOU COULD GO BACK A FEW YEARS AGO AND PICK ME DOESN'T IT. HAHA JUST KIDDING.

I let out a silent laugh, silently wondering about the exact same thing, and plugged my phone into the charging port, made my way down to my bedroom, and got ready for the rest of my day.

Chapter Two

Chase - Three months later

My cell phone let out a shrill ring just as I grabbed my keys from the entryway table. I pocketed my wallet and threw my jacket on just as the phone rang again. I had half a mind to ignore the fucking thing after the day I'd had. I was stressed to the nines about a case I was working on, and then during court this morning I had received a message from Sophie.

As soon as court broke for recess, I listened to her message. She sounded off, and her message was just strange and out of sorts for her, and it left me feeling concerned. I had attempted to call her back, but court had been called back into session, and unfortunately all I could do was quickly message her back and ask her to contact me in a bit. I had yet to hear back from her. The phone rang out again, and this time I pulled it from my pocket and quickly answered it.

"Hello," I barked. I was rushed for time, and even though I was hoping that it was Sophie, I was also hoping this call would be quick.

"You on your way?" my brother, Bryce, questioned.

"Yep, be there in five minutes," I said, grabbing my comfortable old running shoes from the hall closet, slipping my feet into them, and heading out to meet my brothers for our monthly boys' night. I was looking forward to a night of relaxation, beer, and conversation.

By the time I pulled into the parking lot of Ducky's it was pretty full. I found a spot around back of the restaurant, pulled into it, shut the engine off, and went inside. As soon as I opened the doors, I immediately spotted my three brothers sitting in our usual booth in the back. I was just about to walk over when I heard two familiar voices call out to me. I glanced over at the bar and saw both Carly and Delilah waving at me. I flashed them my sexy grin. "Afternoon, ladies."

"What can we get for you today, Chase?" they both called out in unison.

"How about a cold beer, ladies."

"You got it, sexy," Delilah called back, while Carly winked at me.

My brothers sat watching intently as I waved and smiled to half of the women in the bar before I slid into the booth. Within seconds, our usual waitress, Trinity, set my beer down in front of me. She ran her hand over my shoulder and winked. "Wish you would call sometimes. I would love to see you again. It gets pretty lonely at night," she whispered to me.

I glanced at my brothers, praying that none of them had heard her comment, but I knew they had just from the way they were watching me. I smiled at her and took a swig of my beer, trying to ignore what she had said, but instead of walking away, she left her hand on my shoulder.

"I might give you a call, but honestly, I'm really enjoying my alone time right now, Trin." I could tell from the look on her face that I had pretty much crushed her, but I wasn't going to lie; it wasn't my style. It also wasn't my style to get re-involved with a woman if I had no interest in developing it any further. Trinity had been fun during the time we had been involved, but I wasn't interested in anything more with her. I looked to my brothers, each of them staring back at me.

"What the hell, Chase. You've been with all these women in here and you still have the balls to come in here and flirt that way? Do you have a death wish?" Hunter asked.

"Hey, each one of these ladies were and are well aware that I don't want a relationship. I'm upfront about it with them. I'm also upfront and honest in regards to when it ends, it ends. Trinity is just lonely, and besides, no one picked on you when you had your cock in everything that moved in this town."

"First, I didn't have my cock in everything in this town..."

Carter let out a loud laugh. "Oh please, give it a break, would you." He grabbed his scotch and took a drink. "You had your fair share of this town too."

Hunter flipped Carter the finger as we all laughed, then they both shook their heads and took a drink. Bryce looked at me with a shit-eating grin. "It's all right, guys. One of these days, he'll turn around, meet a woman, and his world will spin upside down. You know how it is."

"Yep, and the Chase Malone we all know and love will forever be changed by one pussy." Hunter let out a laugh loud enough to call attention to our table.

"Fuck you all! I'm not like you guys. No way am I settling down. I'm having way too much fun." I grinned.

"Yep, that sounds familiar. I think I said those exact same words right before I meant Autumn," Hunter murmured. "I also believe I said them right to the both of you."

"But then you meet someone, fall in love, and none of these girls will even enter your mind," Carter chimed in, setting his glass down.

"What the hell would you know about it? You married

pretty much the first women you were ever serious about," Bryce smugly replied.

I shook my head, while Carter and Bryce continued to banter back and forth. I opened the menu and looked it over, even though I already knew what I was going to order: two pounds of hot wings—the same thing I ordered every single time we came here. "You fucks don't know what you are missing," I barked out as the three of them were now involved in one of our usual bickering matches.

"Same could be said for you, you know," Carter bit out, seemingly agitated with me.

Trinity approached our table and was halfway through taking our orders when my phone rang. I glanced down and saw Sophie's number sitting on the screen. "And for you, Chase?" she asked, pulling my attention away.

"A pound of hot wings please, Trin," I murmured as my attention quickly focused back on Sophie's number.

"Only a pound?" Carter asked, dumbfounded. "Normally, you're good for at least two."

"Yeah, watching my waistline." I ran my hand over my eight-pack and glanced once again at my phone that was still ringing. "Excuse me, guys, I have to take this," I said, ignoring the murmurs from my brothers. I got up from my seat and headed out the front door.

"Hello," I said as I pushed the door to Ducky's open

and stepped outside into the parking lot, avoiding the group of people heading inside.

"Chase. Sorry to bother you. I know you're probably with your brothers, but my day got kind of crazy after I had called you this morning."

"Hey, yeah it's our usual night out, but it's no bother, Sophie. Sorry I wasn't able to talk earlier. I was in court. I'm glad you called me back. You seemed off in your message. What's up? What's going on?"

Sophie was quiet for a few moments before she cleared her throat. "Do you think you could meet me for dinner tomorrow night? I have something I want to run by you?"

"Is everything okay? It's nothing serious is it?" I could tell from the slight tremor in her voice that whatever she wanted to speak to me about, it was important.

"No, it's nothing bad. I just want to talk to you about something," she assured me.

"Sure, just name the time and place and I will be there." I opened my calendar on my phone to check and make sure I was free.

"The Manor House, tomorrow night at, say, seven."

The Manor House was one of Kings Cove's higher-end steak houses, which made me wonder if everything was indeed okay. "Are you sure everything is okay?" I questioned, wanting to make sure before I got off the phone with her.

"Yeah, I promise you everything is okay. We will talk

tomorrow night. I have to run and finish up a meeting with one of my clients. I'll see you tomorrow at seven."

I could still hear the shake in her voice, but before I had the chance to ask her in a different way if everything was okay, the phone had gone dead. I looked down at my cell phone, wondering what could possibly be so important that she just couldn't tell me over the phone, but a few seconds later, I had shrugged it off and headed back inside. I was quiet as I walked back to our table. Once there, I slid into the booth, checked my watch again, and pocketed my cell phone.

"Was that your hot date for tonight?" Hunter questioned, nodding towards my phone.

"Something like that," I answered, still rather distracted and bothered. "It was Sophie. She wants to meet for dinner tomorrow night. She says she has something she wants to talk to me about. I can't recall a time that she didn't just come out and tell me what was up."

"Oh, *the Sophie*?" Bryce asked.

"Not the unattainable Sophie?" Carter joined in, smirking at Hunter.

I rolled my eyes and took another pull on my beer, doing my best to ignore his comment, and glanced at Hunter who sat there smirking at me. My brothers had always bugged me about Sophie, especially when we had been younger and she had turned me down. Although, unlike those times, this time I didn't laugh or answer any of their questions. When Hunter noticed, he looked at them both and cleared his throat just like our father used to when he wanted us to stop bugging one another.

"What time are you supposed to be meeting her?" he questioned.

"Tomorrow night at seven at The Manor House."

"The Manor House?"

"That is what she said."

"Must be something special. That place isn't cheap." Carter said, "I took Hope there not too long ago. Three hundred and fifty dollars later..."

"Yeah, Autumn's been bugging me to take her there since Hope told her about it. My wallet isn't looking forward to that bill." Hunter and Carter both laughed.

"Well, if you care about me, tell Autumn and Hope not to mention it to Mia." All three of my brothers laughed.

My phone vibrated in my pocket as Carter and Hunter went on discussing dinner prices. I looked down at my phone to see a message from Sophie and glanced at my watch. I feverishly typed out a response to her. I put my phone down and immediately it vibrated, causing me to pick it up again.

"What is it now?" Bryce questioned, as I continued to type out my third response.

"Six-thirty. She wants to meet me a half hour earlier. Something has got to be wrong."

"What the hell is the rush? I mean, she's kept you waiting all these years." Bryce laughed, looking over to Carter and Hunter.

"Man, she hasn't kept me waiting. We are friends. It is possible for me to be friends with a woman," I bit out.

"Sure..." Hunter said before all three of my brothers burst into laughter.

Shortly after I had sent my last text to Sophie, our dinner was dropped onto the table. My mind was so distracted I could barely eat, which was just another thing that my brothers decided to bug me about. I had never been so happy to have my favorite night of the week end.

I drove home in silence, had a hot shower, and crawled into bed, turning the TV on. I was surprised when my phone vibrated and Sophie's name popped up on my screen. As I read her message asking me to meet her yet another half an hour earlier than previously agreed upon, I knew that whatever it was she wanted to talk to me about was important. However, when I asked her once again, she wouldn't even hint at what the issue was.

I shut the light off, shut my phone off, and rolled onto my side and fought to fall asleep.

Chapter Three

Sophie

"I Will Wait" by Mumford and Sons played in my ear as I ran up the last flight of stairs back to my condo. I had completed my nine-mile run in record time today. Out of breath, I leaned against the wall and fumbled with my key, finally inserted it into the lock, and opened the door to my place. I walked in, kicked off my sneakers, removed my headband from my hair, and grabbed a bottle of water from the fridge. I pulled the earbuds from my ears and dropped my iPod onto the table before I made my way down the hall to the washroom. I turned on the shower, making sure the water was the right temperature before I pealed myself out of my workout gear. I'd spent the morning working, and after dealing with a rather testy client, going over his corporate year end, I had decided that I need to get into the gym and work off my stress. The client wasn't the only reason I needed to work off some steam. Dinner with Chase tonight was the other reason.

I stepped into the shower and let the hot water run over my body. As the water beat down on my aching muscles, I tried my best to clear my mind and relax. I dropped two drops of lavender essential oil onto the floor of the shower and took in a deep breath. By the time the water had run cold, I hoped out of the shower and stood in front of the mirror wrapped in a towel. All the hard work of trying to quiet my mind and find my calm had been useless; my mind was more active now than it had been before I had gotten into the shower.

I glanced at my reflection and let out a deep sigh. My mind was busy going over everything that I wanted to talk to Chase about. I had spent the better part of the past week trying to figure out what would be the best way to pitch my idea to him, and after the list of ideas I had made, I still had nothing. I must have gone over fifty or sixty ways today alone on how to even begin the conversation with him tonight before I began to get frustrated.

"Accountants don't pitch people, Sophie," I said aloud to my reflection. The more I thought about it, the more I was beginning to wonder if I wasn't about to make some colossal mistake.

Frustrated with myself, I left the bathroom, walked across the plush carpet in my bedroom, and began sifting through my closet. I needed something conservative yet sexy to wear tonight. I laughed to myself as I started going through my dresses. This is not a date, I thought to myself as I continued going through the dresses that hung in the back of my closet. I was growing frustrated. Accountants *did* have sexy outfits; mine just seemed to be conservative or boring.

I let out a sigh, flipping to the next dress. "Whoa, way too sexy, too sexy, way too conservative, funeral, funeral," I mumbled as I flipped through the dresses that hung in my closet. "Finally...this is perfect!"

I squealed as I pulled out my favorite black cocktail dress and placed it on the bed. I stood back and looked it over. I had only purchased it because it had reminded me of the dress Julia Roberts wore in *Pretty Woman*. I seriously couldn't even remember if I had worn it, but it was perfect for tonight, and I smiled to myself, wandered over to my dresser, and pulled out my only matching black bra and pantie set.

"May as well know I am wearing something sexy underneath..." I mumbled as I slipped into them and then went back to the bathroom and pulled out my makeup bag.

I sat down and brushed my hair, quickly sweeping it

up into a clip on my head and looked at my reflection in the mirror.

"You better be prepared. He is a lawyer, after all," I murmured to myself. "You can't just go in there on a whim. Chase thinks twelve steps ahead of everyone and on everything."

How true that statement was. He would have every single argument against why this was a bad idea, if I knew him, which I did, and he would have them ready within sixty seconds of me spilling the beans. That reason alone was why I needed to have a solid pitch ready and have every answer to every reason why he was going to come up with as to why this was a bad idea.

I looked at myself in the mirror, blew out a breath, and smoothed moisturizer into my skin, then I grabbed the bottle of foundation. "Plus, he specializes in contract law. It's going to be a nightmare, if you aren't prepared," I murmured.

I pumped out a squirt of foundation into the palm of my shaky hand and quickly smoothed that onto my skin, then I reached for my powder compact. Carefully, I smoothed out my foundation, making sure there were no bare spots, and reached for my eyeshadow. My stomach rolled in anticipation of our date, and my hands shook.

This whole meeting in public had been my bright idea. I could have just as easily invited him over for coffee and spoken to him in private about all of this, but no, I was the one who wanted to do this over dinner. I was the one who wanted to do it over dinner in a crowded restaurant. I had never even contemplated what would happen if he flat out refused on the spot, got up and walked out of the restaurant leaving me looking foolish sitting there all alone. How humiliating that would be, I thought. Within seconds of that realization, my stomach rolled. I was so nervous, I seriously wondered if I would even be able to eat anything. Another reason why a public meeting was probably not such a bright idea. I quickly lined my eyes with eyeliner and grabbed my mascara.

"What do I have to offer him?" I wondered out loud. "Nothing about my job is even remotely sexy. I'm a freaking accountant for goodness sakes. I guess I could help him from having to pay too much in tax, and I could definitely keep him out of jail for anything tax related." I looked at my reflection in the mirror, nervously smiled, and then dropped my head in my hands thinking how pathetic I sounded, even to myself.

Perhaps a drink, I thought. Maybe that would make it easier and take the edge off. I got up from my vanity and wandered into the kitchen. I pulled open my liquor cabinet and pulled out the bottle of gin, dropped two ice cubes into my glass, and poured myself a gin and soda. I took a sip of the cool liquid and went back to my vanity and began drying my hair.

Where would we meet, I thought to myself as I

continued to dry my hair. *I guess we could meet here, or perhaps somewhere between our condos would be better.* Perhaps I could pay for a hotel. No, there was no way Chase would meet at a hotel. He was too well-known around town. Okay, so here. He'd have to come here. I didn't even know why I was so concerned about where we would meet. It wasn't as if we had to hide from anyone.

I ran my fingers through my hair, and as soon as it was dry, I shut the switch off on my hairdryer. I ran my brush through it, styling my strands with my fingers, and once I was satisfied, I grabbed the hairspray. As I stood in front of the mirror, looking myself over, I couldn't stop ringing my hands. My stomach still felt uneasy, and the anxiety was building in my chest, making it harder to breathe. I took another sip of gin and soda, praying that the alcohol would kick in and calm some of this anxiety I was feeling. I slipped my dress on and checked the time.

I still had forty-five minutes. I grabbed my glass and went out to the living room, sitting down on the couch. I grabbed my phone and called the restaurant to confirm the reservation time. I felt like I was going crazy. I had just booked the reservation not even twenty-four hours ago, and here I was, paranoid that perhaps I had made it for the wrong date, or the wrong time, or perhaps they didn't mark it down in their book.

I hung up the phone and glanced at my watch. I could get going but didn't really want to arrive too early. I didn't want to seem too eager. I'd rather walk into the restaurant late than be there before him.

I sat back, grabbed my drink and my notepad and pen, took a sip of my drink, and tried my best to come up with some sort of proposal.

Chapter Four

Chase

The sun was directly in my eyes, making it hard to concentrate on the cars in front of me. Twice I had almost rear-ended the car in front of me. I tapped my thumb on the steering wheel to the beat of the music that was blaring through my speakers. I pulled into the parking lot and found a spot, quickly cutting the engine.

I pocketed my keys as I walked up the steps to the doors of the The Manor House and entered in behind the couple in front of me. While I stood waiting to speak with the hostess, I still couldn't help but wonder what the hell Sophie needed. I had not been able to figure out what could be so important that she needed to tell me in person. The urgency in her voice had me worried that something was wrong. Was she sick? Was she in legal trouble? It had driven me crazy most of last night and well into this morning, until I had no choice but to head to the gym and blow off some steam.

"Can I help you?" the young hostess behind the counter asked.

"Reservations for two. Should be under Sophie Lancaster." I watched as she ran her finger down the list of names in front of her, finally stopping and crossing our name off.

"Your table isn't quite ready yet, sir. If you would like, you can have a seat in the bar area, and I'll come and get you once it's ready. Should only be about ten to fifteen minutes."

"Sounds good, thank you." I made my way towards the bar, sitting in the first empty seat I found. I ordered myself a crown and cola and Sophie a gin and soda. The bartender set the drinks down in front of me, and I was passing him a twenty when I felt a hand on my shoulder. I turned to see Sophie standing behind me.

I couldn't help but allow my eyes to run over her. I had never seen her in the dress that she wore, but it hugged her curves perfectly. She smiled at me, and I cleared my throat and stood up. "Here, take a seat," I said, offering her my bar chair.

"Thank you."

"This is for you. Your favorite: gin and soda," I said, moving the glass in front of her and leaning in to kiss her cheek.

Sophie looked up at me, quickly kissed my cheek, and smiled. "You remembered!"

"How could I ever forget? It was the only drink that didn't end up making you hang your head out of my car window every weekend when we were in college," I said, winking at her as we both laughed. Even though we still got out with our college friends once a month, Sophie never drank gin and sodas when we were out anymore and hadn't in years. It had strictly been a college thing.

"That is sadly very true. Although I don't think it's a secret that I still can't hold my liquor very well." She smiled and looked up at me. As soon as I met her eyes, we both took a sip of our drinks. I placed my glass back down on the bar and looked back down to see the smile she had worn was now replaced with a look of nervousness. She was fidgeting with the strap of her clutch that sat neatly tucked in her lap.

"What's up, Soph?" I questioned, downing the rest of my crown and cola and signaling the bartender for another.

"Nothing, why?" she let out a nervous laugh.

"Look at you. You're a nervous mess. You never fidget, and you've just about broken the strap on your clutch."

"I'll be right back. I need to use the ladies' room."

Before I could say anything, she had jumped up and dashed through the crowd over to the washrooms. Minutes passed, and I was beginning to get worried.

I glanced down at my watch to try and determine how long she had been gone when the hostess came to tell me that our table was ready. I was about to ask her to hold the table when Sophie finally reappeared. Something was up. She didn't have her usual glow. The look on her face reminded me of the time we had been hanging at her parents' house and we had accidentally broken her mother's antique lamp. It had been a present from her father. I smiled inwardly to myself as I remembered her standing with her hands behind her back trying to tell her parents what had happened.

"Our table is ready," I said as she got closer.

"Awesome. Just awesome," she mumbled. I frowned as I watched as she picked up her glass and waved for me to go first, but I refused and instead waved my hand, signaling for her to go first. Once she was in front of me, I placed my hand on the small of her back and together we walked to the table.

I was hoping to find out immediately what was going on, but once we were seated and the hostess had left, Sophie had conveniently buried her face in her menu. I frowned, and even though it was killing me, I didn't say anything while we looked over the menu. We had both settled on our choices by the time the waitress had returned to drop a fresh basket of bread onto the center of our table. We ordered quickly, and I reached in and cut a piece of bread for Sophie, passing it to her. She barely made eye contact with me as she reached over and took it from my hand. Her odd behavior was seriously beginning to get to me.

I sat forward, crossed my arms in front of me, and leaned on the table. "The suspense is killing me here, Soph. What was it you needed to talk to me about?" I asked, taking a sip of my Crown and Coke, while she buttered her bread and took a bite.

She looked around the room, ignoring me. I let out a breath and started slicing the loaf of bread again. "You know I adore you, right?" her soft voice questioned.

I looked up at her, pausing from cutting the loaf of bread. "Yes, of course, and I you." I winked, trying to lighten the mood, but she completely ignored me.

"And you know I'm not getting any younger, right?"

I frowned. "Neither am I."

"And historically you've always come through for me." She swallowed hard, setting her bread down on the side plate. "No matter what."

"Okay, let's cut to the goods here, Soph. What's going on? Are you okay? Are you sick? In legal trouble?" The way she was carrying on, I feared she had some sort of terminal illness.

I proceeded to cut more slices off the loaf of bread.

"Well, it's just I want a baby, and I want you to be the father," she blurted out.

My head shot up. I looked at Sophie, who sat across from me still chewing on her bread as if she had just told me who won the hockey game on Friday night. I swallowed hard, not sure I believed what I had just heard.

"Did you hear me?" she asked, waving her hand in front of my face.

"You—you aren't getting any younger, and you...you want my swimmers?" That was all I could get out before I felt a searing hot pain in the hand that was holding onto the loaf of bread. I glanced down and saw blood starting to soak into the white napkin I was using to hold onto the bread with.

"Shit," I mumbled, pulling my hand towards me.

"Oh my God, Chase." Sophie jumped up and grabbed her napkin and my hand and quickly pressed the napkin against the cut, gently but firmly squeezing. She held it for a couple of seconds, and then pulled the napkin away to inspect the cut. I sat there not knowing what to say or do, completely shocked at what she had just blurted out. "It's okay. I don't think you need stitches or anything. Just hold the napkin tight, and the bleeding should stop," she said, continuing to examine my hand.

"You want my swimmers?" I mumbled, completely forgetting about the cut on my hand.

As the waitress approached our table, Sophie asked for

a band-aid, and I raised my glass, signaling for another Crown and Coke. Hell, at this point, they could just bring me the entire bottle of Crown. My appetite had fled after what Sophie had asked, but I sure as hell needed to get loaded.

I couldn't believe my ears. Sophie, the girl who had told me no all those years ago, now wanted...a baby...my baby. I felt like I was going to faint. I swallowed hard. "Why me?"

"Well, honestly, I'm thirty, and there is absolutely no one on the horizon for even a date, never mind a relationship that would lead to a baby anytime soon. Second, I've known you all my life. I'm comfortable with you. You have a good work ethic, you're smart, not to mention attractive. You are caring, kind, and considerate, and I seriously can't think of a better father for my child." She let out a deep breath and brought her glass to her lips.

"I see."

The waitress appeared carrying our food and set our meals down in front of us. The craving I'd had all day for bacon-wrapped filet mignon smothered in onions and mushrooms was now long gone. I stared down at the perfectly cooked steak, my mind spinning in circles, while Sophie was busy cutting a piece of steak into bite-sized pieces. She popped a piece into her mouth, the nervous look now gone as she chewed. I didn't know what to say. I felt as if I were in the middle of a very bad dream.

I had no idea how long I had sat there watching her eat, but the next thing I knew, she had cleared her plate while mine was still full and getting cold.

"Are you okay? Aren't you going to eat?" she asked, looking a bit worried.

I picked up my glass of Crown and Cola and took a large drink. I shook my head and set the glass back down. "I'm not really all that hungry," I mumbled.

She nodded and pulled the napkin from her lap, moved her plate to the side, and placed her arms on the table. "Well, now that I have laid everything out, do you have an answer for me?" Her eyes filled with hope.

I looked at her. She was expecting an answer right now? It was as if she had asked me to pick something up from the store for her, not give her a baby. I let out a breath, looking down at my plate, and then at my napkin-swaddled hand.

"I'll have to think about it, Sophie. This is a big decision, and one I am not going to take lightly."

The excitement in her eyes had disappeared and was now replaced with disappointment, and I certainly didn't like seeing it; however, there was no way I could just commit to something like this.

"Sir, was there something wrong with your meal?" our waitress asked as she picked up Sophie's plate.

I shook my head, afraid to speak.

"Would you like that plate boxed up?" the waitress asked as she dropped our bill on the table.

I nodded. As soon as she had cleared our plates away, I reached for the check folder, but Sophie grabbed it first. "I'll get this," she said and opened the folder.

"No, give it to me please," I insisted, holding my hand out, but she shook her head and slid her credit card into the slot and set it beside her at the edge of the table. She kept her head down, ignoring me, and sifted through her purse.

We sat in silence, Sophie going through her purse, and me thinking about how I could have done things differently. It seemed to take forever, but finally the bill had been paid, and I now sat with my takeover package in front of me. Sophie quickly put her credit card back into her wallet and stood. "When can I expect to hear from you?" she questioned.

I thought for a second. I didn't want to jeopardize our friendship, so I answered with the first thing that came to my mind. "Next week?"

She leaned in and kissed me on the cheek, smiled shyly at me, and turned and walked away. I sat back down at the table, trying to grasp what the hell had just happened. I was at a loss for words and really wasn't sure I should get behind the wheel.

I pulled my phone from my pocket and dialed Hunter's number. It was almost eight. I knew he was probably putting the kids to bed, but I needed my brother. The phone rang five times before an out-of-breath Hunter answered. "Hey, man, what's going on?"

"Hey, listen, can you come pick me up?"

"Ah, why? Is everything okay?"

"I'll explain when you get here."

"Where is here?"

"The Manor House," I choked out and hung up the phone before he could refuse.

Chapter Five

Sophie

I left the restaurant and walked across the parking lot, feeling completely and utterly defeated. The whole night had been an utter disaster. Not only did I make a complete ass of myself, but I also injured my best friend. That cut looked pretty bad. I crawled into the driver's seat of my car, threw my purse on the floor, and started the engine. I sat there for a few moments trying to center myself and finally pulled out of the spot.

I blew out a breath as I pulled up to a stoplight. The feeling of humiliation continued to sink in. There was no coming back from this now. Why hadn't I really thought through the entire conversation? I slammed my hand down on the steering wheel, annoyed with myself. I really didn't know what I was expecting. Had I expected him to be like he had always been: eager to help me with whatever dilemma I had been facing? Perhaps that was just it. Perhaps I had expected him to turn around and instantly agree. Instead, he had cut his hand, hadn't eaten dinner, and barely said two words to me the entire time we had been at the restaurant. He also had drank one too many Crown and Cokes, and I just left him there to fend for himself.

I should have turned around and went back to get him, make sure he got home safe, but instead I turned the radio on and proceeded through the green light, the guilt of the night sinking farther into me. What if I had just ruined our lifetime friendship? My stomach sank at the thought of no longer having Chase around. The thought of not having him in my life nearly made me sick.

A blaring horn pulled me from the thought, and I immediately noticed I was driving into the oncoming lane. I quickly righted my vehicle and drove a ways down the road to my apartment.

I locked the door behind me, turning on lights as I entered my condo. I kicked off my shoes, dropped my purse on the floor, and slipped out of my coat, hanging it in the small closet. My mind was still racing a mile a minute over how I could have done things so differently.

I grabbed the remote from the table and turned the

TV on, drowning out the quiet of my apartment, and wandered down the hall to my bedroom. I looked at myself in the full-length mirror, my makeup slightly smudged now from the few tears that I hadn't even realized had fallen on my way home. I turned away from my reflection and unzipped my dress, letting it fall to a pile in the middle of the room. I slipped out of my bra and panties and put on my sweats that were lying on the bottom of my bed. I needed to relax. I quickly washed my face, put my hair up in a messy bun, and shut the light off.

Time had passed once I had found something on TV, and I now lay on the couch trying to get lost in an episode of *Friends*; however, the only thing on my mind was how I had foolishly proposed my bright idea to Chase. Over and over, the words I had so casually dropped ran through my mind like a bad nightmare. Perhaps I should have been more prepared than I was. Perhaps I should have written them all down to present to him in a more business-like way. He may have been more receptive if I'd had everything in a nice presentation folder, like one of his legal briefs he had shown me numerous times. Nevertheless, the damage was done, and it was out in the open now, and all I could do was wait. Wait for his answer, either yes or no, or perhaps he would say "Get away from me, Sophie, and don't bother coming around again." Honestly, I wasn't even sure what it was I expected him to say. Was I really expecting him to drop everything and say yes? Or was the answer he gave me more the one I was expecting?

I reached for the phone and relaxed back against the pillow behind me and debated calling Chase and apologizing. I dropped my head back against the pillow and pinched the bridge of my nose, trying to gather up the courage to dial Chase's number. Instead, I let out a sigh and called Jenna. I needed to talk to her, but the phone just rang and rang. I was just about to give up when I heard her answer completely out of breath.

"It's about time you called me!" Jenna blurted into the phone. "You said you would call by seven."

"Yeah, sorry, I lost track of time. What were you doing? You're all out of breath. Oh my God, I didn't...I didn't interrupt anything, did I?" I questioned, my face heating.

Jenna broke out in laughter. "Good Lord, girl, Matt isn't even home from the office yet. Besides, if you think I would answer the phone in the middle of that, you are crazier than I originally thought. If you must know, I was running on the treadmill. Get your head out of the gutter. I'm trying to be good this month. I fell off the wagon last month going to Aroma Mocha almost every weekend, and my waistline is showing it."

"Girl you are crazy. You're perfect!" I glanced at my watch. "Besides, it's almost ten. You should be in your sweats relaxing."

"Ha, tell that to my jeans, and I'm in my sweats. Also, running is a form of relaxation I guess." She giggled. "So what took you so long to call me? You could have saved me from all this torture tonight, and we could have gone and gotten ice cream."

I let out a small laugh. "I had somewhere I needed to be after work."

"You had somewhere you needed to be? Where? You basically live at the office, and when you aren't there you are at home."

"Well, I had something to do after work. I just got home about a half an hour ago."

"You had something to do after work. Why are you being so vague? You tell me everything. So, do you care to share with your good ol' friend? Stop making me have to try and guess."

I giggled. This was just like Jenna; she always had to know where I was. "I had dinner plans."

"Oooh, anyone I know?"

I let out a deep breath. "If you must know, I had dinner with Chase." We both grew quiet until I cleared my throat. "I did it." I couldn't hold back any longer.

"You did what?" she asked curiously.

After that afternoon at the coffee shop, and after my breakup with Roger, we had talked at great lengths about me asking one of our close friends to be the father of my child. I had been adamant at first, but she had been totally supportive and kept telling me to just go for it.

"I asked Chase to be the father of my child."

I heard a gurgle and a cough on the other end of the phone as Jenna choked on whatever it was she was drinking. "You did what?"

"You heard me."

"Well, what did he say?"

I let out a little laugh, remembering his face as I had asked him. "Well, it didn't go as smoothly as I thought it would. First, he sliced his hand open."

"What? No, I mean, what did he say to your question?"

"He said he would think about it."

"Oh my! And you told him everything, right?"

I let out a sigh. Perhaps if had I told him everything, his answer might have been different. "Well, if he hadn't been bleeding all over the place I might have, but no, I didn't. Do you think I should have told him everything?"

Jenna started to laugh. "Sophie, it may have helped your case if you had. Don't you think?"

"Perhaps. I don't know, maybe this really is a bad idea."

"Why do you say that?"

I laughed. "If you had seen his face, you'd be thinking the same thing. I can only imagine what the other guys would have said if I had asked one of them."

"Girl, you are crazy."

"No, I'm serious. I also keep thinking that if I had just gone in there with everything written down and in a true proposal style, he may have looked at the entire situation differently. Maybe more like a business deal."

"Perhaps if you had delivered all the goods, then he might have jumped at the chance. Listen, I've got to go. Matt just walked through the door. Call me later and we will talk, okay?"

"All right, night."

"Seriously, Soph, talk to him, give him all the goods."

"Good night, Jenna!"

I hung up the phone and turned the TV off. Shutting the lights off, I grabbed my cell phone and headed to the bedroom. I crawled into bed and lay facing the floor-to-ceiling window, looking at the lights of the city like I did every night. My mind was still running over everything that had happened tonight. Jenna was right. If I had given him all the details up front, perhaps his answer might have been yes. However, I was glad I had held back because he might have cut his hand off too. I giggled at the thought. I grabbed my cell phone from the side table and quickly opened a text message to Chase.

I typed feverishly at first, then decided to delete everything and began again. I couldn't just come out and say it like I was planning to. I had no clue where he was. He could have been behind the wheel of his car, God forbid.

Besides, I didn't want him to get the information through a text either.

ME: Would you be able to meet me tomorrow for lunch. At the risk of sounding like those infomercials we used to watch as kids...but wait! There's more...but wait, there is more, and I want another chance to discuss this with you.

I blew out a breath and placed my cell phone on the table, closed my eyes, and tried to fall into a deep sleep.

Chapter Six

Chase

I sat on the hood of my car and looked up at the dark sky in utter shock. I still couldn't believe what had transpired tonight. My best friend had asked me to be the father of her child. I shook my head and ran my hand through my hair. I glanced down to the bag of cold food that sat beside me, my stomach letting out a loud grumble. I wasn't sure if I was hungry or if I was going to be sick.

I let out a huff and pulled my phone from my pocket. I checked the last text I had received from Hunter and saw it was over an hour ago. I was just about to message him to find out where he was when a car I recognized pulled into the parking lot and in beside mine. I hopped off the hood of my car, grabbed the bag of food, and pulled the passenger door open on Hunter's car.

"It's about damn time!" I said, crawling into the front seat and pulling my seatbelt across my body.

"Yeah, well, Autumn needed help getting the kids to bed. It was bath night. It's not like I can expect her to deal with them all on her own. What the hell happened to your hand?" Hunter questioned, staring down at my napkin-wrapped hand. "And what's wrong with your car?" he asked and nodded towards my vehicle.

"Nothing."

"You called me out here for nothing? What the hell you do to your hand?"

"Not for nothing. I had a little too much to drink, and this..." I said, raising my hand. "I cut myself while slicing a loaf of bread." I shrugged.

"Jesus," he muttered under his breath as he watched me place my leftovers bag between us.

"What?" I questioned.

"Leftovers? From the sounds of things, the portions are small there. Carter said he was still hungry when he left, and you come out with leftovers? Was it at least a good meal?"

I shrugged. "Honestly, I have no idea!"

"What do you mean you have no idea? You were just there for dinner."

"If you must know, the bag contains my meal. I

couldn't eat. I totally lost my appetite after I cut my hand. Here, if you want you can take it home and share it with Autumn. She'd probably enjoy it," I said holding the bag out to him. I glanced over at my car and locked my doors with my remote fob.

I didn't even need to look at my brother because I could feel him staring at me as if I had lost my mind. "Are you feeling all right? You're acting strange."

"Can we just go?" Hunter continued watching me for a second, not saying anything. "Please?"

Hunter didn't argue. Instead, he revved the engine and put the car into reverse and sped out of the parking lot. We had driven about two blocks and were stopped at a stoplight. He was tapping his thumb on the steering wheel and watching a lady walk across the street when he cleared his throat. "Care to talk about it?" he asked once the light turned green and he started driving through the inter-section.

I threw my head back against the headrest, and with my eyes closed I mumbled, "Sophie wants to borrow my sperm." I blew out a breath and tried to calm myself down, but the car came to an abrupt stop, and a horn blared out from behind us. "Hunter, what the hell!"

"Sorry about that, but did I hear you right?"

"Yeah, you heard me. Sophie, she wants a baby, and she asked me to father the child." I still couldn't get her voice out of my mind—or the look on her face as she had asked me. The beginning of the night she had been so distraught, but once she asked me, she had appeared to be confident yet completely hopeful that I would do it.

"So like you'd whack off in a cup and pass it over to her?"

"I guess so. I haven't a clue. I cut my hand, and, well, then I started drinking, and the rest of the night went to shit. I could barely even remember my name let alone have any type of real conversation on the matter."

Hunter let out a loud laugh. "That's fucking awesome. So what did you tell her?"

I sat there trying to remember exactly what I had said. All I could remember was the look on her face, the look that I had let her down. There had never been another time in my life that I had remembered ever seeing her face look like that when it came to me. It haunted me. I cleared my throat. "I didn't say anything. I couldn't. I was so shocked that, no matter how much time had passed, I could barely put two words together. Once I gathered myself together enough, I told her I'd think about it. She left looking so defeated."

"Well, you could always negotiate. I mean, you do practice contract law. It's a sterile transaction, right? So slap a contract together, have her sign, and be done with it. I mean, seriously, this is simple. You're making it more difficult than it needs to be. Look at it logically."

"Can you pull over?" I mumbled, undoing my seatbelt, and reaching for the door handle.

"Pull over? What the hell for?"

I couldn't wait. Instead, I rolled down the window and stuck my head out, throwing up right down the side of Hunter's new BMW. My stomach was still swirling as I pulled my head back in the car and put the window up. "Sorry about that. You might want to drive through that car wash over there," I said, pointing to the one across the street. "I'll pay."

"Damn right you'll pay. Jesus, Chase, this is a brand new car."

"Sorry, man."

Hunter began laughing. "It reminds me of when we were younger."

Hunter pulled into the car wash, and we sat in utter silence as we drove through. I sat facing straight ahead, focusing on the movement of the brushes as the whole night played out again in my mind. "Perhaps you should eat something?" Hunter said, pulling back out onto the street and continuing to make his way towards my condo.

"I'm really not hungry."

"All right, so, what did she say exactly? I need all the details."

My phone vibrated in my pocket. I let out a breath, pulling my phone out and looking at the screen.

"Fuck me," I murmured, shoving my phone back in my pocket.

"What?" Hunter asked, pulling into the parking lot of my condo and putting the car into park.

"That was Sophie."

"And?"

"She wants to have lunch with me tomorrow. She says there is more, and she wants to discuss it with me in person, and I think I'm gonna be sick again," I said, opening the car door and crawling out just in time to toss my cookies on the edge of the parking lot.

Hunter chuckled and rolled down the car's window. "Here, don't forget your food," he said, holding up the bag.

"Keep it. Thanks for picking me up." I held my hand over my stomach and waved. Once he pulled from the parking lot, I walked to the main entrance, punched in the security code, and headed up to my condo.

Chapter Seven

Sophie

I'd woken early after a rather restless night of sleep. I had tossed and turned, constantly checking to see if Chase had answered my text – he hadn't. I'd rolled out of bed before my alarm with a bad headache, a bad case of bed head, and practically everything in my body aching. I took a hot shower, popped two pain pills, and got ready for work, leaving the condo with bagel and coffee in hand.

I took my usual route to my office and decided to make a pit stop down by the waterfront. I parked the car, grabbed my coffee, and took a walk down the pier. I needed to try and forget what had happened last night before I got into the office. I would never be able to get through my day, if my mind wasn't clear.

I sat down on a bench, sipped my coffee, and watched the boats leaving the harbor. It was a beautiful day, the sun was shining, the birds chirping, and I took in a deep breath of fresh morning air. While I sipped on my coffee, I watched couples walk along the water's edge, holding hands. I smiled to myself, and once my cup was empty, I got up and made my way back to my car, glancing at my watch.

I pushed the heavy door open and walked into the lobby of my office. I was surprised to see the waiting room as full as it was. I had figured it would still be quiet at this time, and that was when I saw one of my clients was sitting waiting for me. I glanced at my watch as I made my way to my office, and then up to the clock on the wall, and realized my watch had stopped. The place was packed because *I* was the one who was running late. Almost forty minutes late, to be exact. Certainly not the way I wanted to start my day.

I set up my computer in record time and pulled the client file and immediately called them in, apologizing profusely.

A lot of conversation and two hours later, I walked back into my office and picked up the client file that still remained on my desk. That made two appointments down, and even though the day started out rocky, I was feeling surprisingly good, and then I looked to the stack of files that sat on my to-be-done pile. A surge of stress ran through me, and I shuddered at the thought of all I still had left in front of me for today.

"Hey, girl. I'm on my way to refill my cup. Did you want a coffee?" I heard Carol ask as she stopped just inside of my door. She leaned against my door, looking over to the corner of my desk where my work sat. "Looks like you might need one, considering your workload today."

"That would be wonderful, and I have a feeling that I will be taking half this stack home. I just spent an hour with Mr. Leeman and Mr. Sage. Oh, and did you know that Mr. Sage does not like it if you are late," I said, rolling my eyes.

"Ah, yes, Mr. Sage. Say no more, my dear. That alone calls for one *strong* cup of coffee that you should have had prior to the next appointment." We both laughed as she reached for my cup, and then carried on down the hall.

I walked around and sat back down in my chair and opened up the next file that sat on top of the pile. I was going over the notes from our last meeting when Carol set the cup of coffee on my desk. "Thank you! You're a saint," I said, letting out a breath and smiling up at her.

"No worries. Good luck with the rest of your day. I have a boardroom meeting I have to get to."

"Have fun with that."

"You betcha." Carol winked and disappeared from my office.

I glanced at the clock on my desk and went back to reading over the file. I was glad to see I had a few hours before my next meeting, which meant I had plenty of time to get prepared, I thought to myself. I took a sip of coffee and began reading over the client file in front of me.

A good twenty minutes had passed, and I had just gotten deep into file when my cell phone vibrated across my desk, causing me to jump. My heart sped up a little when I saw Chase's name on my screen. As I answered, my stomach did one of those excited but nervous little flips.

"Good morning." I did my best to keep my voice upbeat. I didn't want Chase to think I was nervous to talk with him, but the truth was, my heart was pounding out of my chest.

"Morning. I'm sorry to bother you at work, but I got your message and was hoping that perhaps you still wanted to meet for lunch today."

I glanced down at my watch, and then to my schedule, noting I had time between eleven and one free. "Yep, how is eleven?" I questioned.

"Eleven works fine."

"Where did you want to meet?"

"How about The Manor House, and would you be able to do me a favor and pick me up on your way?" He chuckled.

I frowned. He'd had his car last night. I'd seen it. "Sure. Your car in the shop?"

Chase let out a breath. "No, it's still at the restaurant. Hunter came and picked me up last night. I was in a little bit of shock, not to mention I'd had too much to drink, and my best friend left me high and dry."

I let out a little giggle. "Yeah, I'm sorry about that. Guess I will see you in an hour or so."

"Sounds good. Oh, and, Soph, I'm looking forward to finishing our little talk today."

"Yes, of course. I'll see you soon." I hung up the phone and did my best to ignore the funny feeling in the pit of my stomach as I tried to dive back into the file in front of me. My stomach rolled in anticipation of talking to Chase, and I found it harder to concentrate the more I tried. After ten minutes, I grabbed my legal pad and jotted down some things I wanted to make sure I brought up to Chase. I wasn't about to blow another chance with him. I needed him to realize that I was serious about this.

I saw a few drops of rain on my windshield as I pulled up outside of Malone Law. Chase stood on the sidewalk and waved when he saw my car pull up. He looked just as tired and worn down as I felt. I waved as he approached my car, my stomach doing that anxious little flip again. To say I was nervous was an understatement. Since he had called, I had been absolutely useless at work, and even working on the list of things I wanted to mention to him had been of no help. I quickly tucked the legal pad between my seat and console so that he couldn't see it when he climbed in.

He opened the car door and climbed in, doing up his seat belt before he turned and looked at me. "Hey! How are you?" he mumbled, giving me a nervous smile.

"I'm okay. How are you?"

"Okay." I swallowed hard and pulled away from the curb and headed towards The Manor House. Chase was oddly quiet on the drive, looking out the window as we made our way the five city blocks to the restaurant. I pulled into the parking lot and right up beside Chase's car and cut the engine.

We walked side by side into the restaurant, neither of us saying anything. The tension between us was unbearable, and all I kept thinking to myself was that I was the one who had created this tension. Me and my silly ideas.

Within ten minutes, we were seated at the back of the restaurant, bread basket sitting between us on the table, while the waitress was waiting to take our drink orders.

"I'll have a soda water with lemon," I said, looking to Chase.

"Crown and Coke." He coughed into his hand.

"Um, how about just a coke? I don't want a repeat of last night." I giggled.

Chase rolled his eyes and dismissed the waitress. As soon as she had walked away, he looked over to me. "I'm fine, you know. I'll be fine." He opened the menu in front of him.

I stuck my head into my menu and sat staring at the page, the names of the dishes eventually all blurring together. I was beginning to doubt if I could indeed go through with this whole thing again, after what had happened last night. I sat there trying hard to find something that I wanted to eat, and that was when my worst fear entered my mind. What if he said no? I really didn't know how I would react to that answer.

Chase slapped his menu shut, causing me to jump and draw my attention to him. He reached for the bread, but I quickly swatted his hand away. "Let me." I grabbed the knife from the table and took the bread, cutting it into pieces.

"How is your hand anyways?" I asked.

"It's okay," he said, looking down at his bandaged hand and reached for a piece of bread.

"I felt awful that you cut yourself."

Chase shrugged as he buttered his bread and took a bite.

"All right, so back to what we were talking of last night," I said, finally putting the knife down and grabbing a piece of bread for myself.

"Yes, about that. I have a few things that I want to say," he said, clearing his throat, but I put my hands up to stop him.

"Before you say anything, you should know I want to do this natural," I bit out as he buttered his second piece of bread, fearing he may stab himself with the butter knife.

"What? Childbirth? Of course, both Carter and Hunter have said that Heather and Hope have said they wouldn't have done it any other way, so I can totally understand that."

I shook my head and took a drink of my soda water before continuing. "Um, no, not childbirth. Well, no, yes childbirth, but making the baby. Thought perhaps we should start here first. I also don't want you to worry. I won't hold you accountable for anything."

Chase looked around the restaurant and then back to me. So far so good, I thought to myself. *He hasn't cut himself or passed out yet.*

"Okay. Go on." He swallowed hard.

"Okay, so this is what I was thinking. You'd spend the week at my place. Now if you stay in October, which is next week, I've counted everything out, and if everything goes according to my plan, then I will be good to work right through tax season before the baby comes. However, it has to be the first week of the month. One week earlier or later, and it will mess everything up."

Chase finished chewing and took a drink, placing his glass down on the table. "I see you've really thought this out."

I nodded. "I have. I'm very serious about this, and that also is exactly the right time. I've been tracking my cycle, and next week is the most optimal time for me to get pregnant."

Chase was just about to say something when our food was placed in front of us. His eyes met mine as the waitress announced each dish and finally walked away. We both dug into our plates and ate in silence. Once our plates were cleared and the bill was delivered to the table, Chase sat forward.

"Listen, Sophie, I'm still going to think about this. I will have a decision to you in a couple of days. Does that sound okay?"

I nodded. I felt confident that I had laid everything out on the table. Chase hadn't fainted or cut himself, and I felt satisfied and hopeful with his answer. I went to reach for the bill, but Chase grabbed it first. "You got last night. The least I can do is get lunch." He winked.

"All right, I've got to go," I said, glancing down at my watch. "I have a client in a half hour. I'll talk to you soon."

Chase stood as I stood, and unlike last night, this time he kissed me on the cheek before I walked away.

Chapter Eight

Chase

I had been trying to type out this damn email for the past hour and still had yet to get the tone of it correct. I hit delete, wiping the entire contents of my email, and slammed my fists on my desktop and began typing again. The sooner I could get this finished, the quicker I could get home and unwind, and unwinding was exactly what I needed. I was about three sentences into the email when I once again hit delete and began all over again.

"Hey, man, you all set?" Hunter appeared in my doorway, leaning against the doorjamb, shoving the last of what looked like a muffin into his mouth.

"Yep, all the loose ends are tied finally. I was just trying to get out one last email for the day, but I can't seem to get the wording correct."

Hunter pulled the chair out on the other side of my desk and sat down across from me with a smug smile. "Things still bothering you, are they?" He grinned.

I nodded. That was an understatement. I'd barely slept in two days. "How are Autumn and the girls? Did she enjoy my dinner the other night?"

"She did, and everyone is good."

"Great! I really miss those angels. I should drop by and visit soon." I shut my laptop in frustration and placed it in the bottom drawer of my desk and looked to Hunter who was still smiling away. "I'll just write the damn email tomorrow morning," I said more out of frustration than anything else.

"What's up? Did you need something before I leave?"

"Just wondering how you made out with your dilemma? Bryce said you went to see her for lunch."

I was just about to answer when Carter and Bryce walked into my office and each took a seat on the couch. I paused. I wasn't sure if I wanted to share this entire situation with everyone. Hunter already knew, so it was a little different sharing it with him. However, I had to remember these were my brothers, and there wasn't much that any of us didn't share with one another. I swallowed hard, trying to decide if I should tell everyone or keep my mouth shut.

"What dilemma are you facing now?" Carter asked, squeezing the spot between his eyes.

"Perhaps he's been mesmerized by that pussy we were talking about two weeks ago." Bryce and Carter both chuckled.

I glanced at Bryce and Carter and back to Hunter who knew the truth. As Carter and Bryce sat there laughing, I was getting more and more irritated, and before I could stop them, the words just fell from my mouth without a care as to what they thought. "Sophie wants to borrow my sperm."

Bryce and Carter both looked at me as if I had spoken another language. "What?" Carter sat forward, resting his forearms on his knees, totally interested in what I had to say next.

"Sophie, she wants a baby and she asked me to um..."

"So like you'd whack off in a cup and pass it over to her. That sounds fucking exciting." Bryce laughed, elbowing Carter, who also began laughing.

I laughed more to myself. "No, not exactly. At first, I thought she was kidding, but now she has proposed seven days of no-strings-attached sex." I ran my hands through my hair.

"Fuck me. You may just be the luckiest bastard alive," Bryce commented. "Sophie is hot as fuck, a little uptight, but I bet once you get her going, she is kinky as fuck too," he said, raising his eyebrows.

"That's enough," I bit back, glaring at my brother. It wasn't that the thought hadn't crossed my mind. Actually, it had crossed my mind many times. My tone was more because he, too, was thinking that exact same thing, or perhaps had in the past.

"What did you tell her?" Hunter asked, trying to pull my attention away from Bryce.

"To be honest, I still haven't answered yet. I was once again so shocked, I didn't know what to say, so I told her I'd think about it."

Each one of my brothers looked at me as if I had lost my mind. "Whoa, hold on a second. A girl gives you permission to screw her, no strings, and you don't jump at the chance?" Bryce questioned. "Are you feeling all right? I think you might be sick."

"Yes, I'm feeling fine," I said, getting up out of my chair and pacing across my office. "Oh, I know you don't believe this, but I do have a conscience. I do respect women, and I don't want to do anything that will jeopardize our friendship."

Bryce roared with laughter. "Jesus, that is the funniest thing I have heard all day."

Carter chuckled and stood up and walked towards the door. "I've got to get home to Hope and the kids. We're headed to the zoo tomorrow, and I promised them we'd go and stay overnight and make a weekend of it. Hunter, Bryce, I'll see you later.

Chase, good luck." He chuckled again and walked out the door.

"See you Monday," Hunter said and turned back to face me. As soon as Carter was gone, Bryce came and sat in the empty chair on the other side of my desk.

"So, you have a conscience. Could have fooled us." Bryce laughed, bringing us all back to our conversation.

"Shut up. She's one of my best friends. What would you do?"

"Oh, so that makes it different than every other woman out there? And what would I do? I jump at the fucking chance."

"Yes, it does make a difference," I mumbled, ignoring his other comment.

"What are you afraid of, that she may not like your piggish ass afterward?" Bryce bit out. Bryce had stayed with me for a bit last year before he met Mia. He, of all of my brothers, knew exactly how I was.

I stopped pacing and looked over at Bryce. He had pretty much hit it on the head. What if, by doing this, we totally ruined the relationship we already had with each other? We basically spoke every day in one way or another, we hung out on weekends, vacationed with the same group of people in the summer, and I already knew that not having her in my life or her not speaking to me would probably kill me.

"That's exactly it." Bryce laughed when I didn't

respond immediately. "You're afraid."

"Can I not share anything with you asses? I don't know what the hell to do. I've never been in this position before."

"Do whatever you think you should." Bryce shrugged, looking at his watch. "I've got to run too. We are expecting Mia's brother and his family this weekend. She'll kill me if I'm not home on time tonight, and since I'm already late, I'm gonna have to make it up to her. See you next week." He waved as he walked out of my office and soon he, too, was gone.

"Hunter, what would you do?" I asked, trying to get some kind of feedback from someone older and wiser— and perhaps a little more mature.

"Honestly?"

"Yes."

He blew out a breath and placed his hands behind his head. He took a few minutes and thought, and then took a deep breath. "Well, I'd have to consider a lot of things."

"Like?"

"What my relationship with said person is and what it might become afterward. So I get where you are coming from on that front. I mean things are going to work out one of two ways: either everything will go back to the way it is now, or the worst, this will drive a rift right between you. You need to figure out how comfortable you would be with that last aspect. You also need to think about protecting yourself. I mean we as a company have a shit-tonne to lose if you go through with this, and then she wants to come after you financially."

"I'm not worried about that. Sophie is in a good place, and I've known her my entire life. Hell, we've all known her. I don't think she is doing this in any way to be vindictive."

"Neither do I, but the stress of dealing with a child alone can do a lot of funny things to people. What happens if she falls in love with you and you don't return the feelings, or you get married and she resents you forever and comes after you. You need to think of all of these things. I mean, you are right, we have known her all her life. Now, on the other hand, you also need to figure out what would happen if you end up wanting more."

"I won't," I immediately replied.

Hunter chuckled at my quick and immediate answer and rubbed the back of his neck. "Listen, I know I'm in a way different place than you are currently, but when I found out Autumn was pregnant, something in me changed. It was like a switch. Suddenly, I wanted to see my baby be born and grow up, and it killed me when she pushed me away. What if you feel the same way and she wants nothing to do with you?"

"Seriously? I'm a donor, nothing more," I bit out.

"So, then you're telling me you're going to do it?"

I looked at my brother. Hunter had brought up great

points, and I'd given zero thought to how I might feel about the entire process, especially how I might feel afterward. I'd also given zero thought to what would happen if she wanted more. I blew out a breath and dropped my head back and stopped and thought for a second. I hadn't really thought about any of the things he'd brought up. All I'd seen was the hurt in her eyes when she walked away from me. I'd seen it before caused by others, and I'd seen happiness, and honestly, I liked seeing the second better. I just wanted to do whatever it took to see that happiness in her eyes again.

"All I'm saying is be careful and be prepared for what you might not expect. Sophie has lived in Kings Cove her entire life, and she isn't going anywhere."

"What is that supposed to mean, she isn't going anywhere?"

"Well, it means that one day, after all this is done with, you will probably run into her on the street. Your son or daughter will be with her. The part that will hurt the most will be the fact that they won't even know who you are when you run into them, but you will. He or she will just think you are nothing more than an acquaintance that their mother knows, but you're going to know. I just want you to think and be fully prepared for how that might feel."

I sat there considering what he had just said. I knew there was a lot of truth in what he was saying. I had seen what a mess he had been over the whole Autumn situation. I blew out a breath.

"Oh, and what if she ends up wanting child support? That can end up being an entirely different can of worms. We work in the law field. Ask Carter the shit he's seen people pull. It will definitely open your eyes."

I nodded. He was right. "What do you think I should do?"

"If you are absolutely sure that you're really going to be finished with this situation after the deed is done, then form a contract and make her sign an NDA," Hunter said, crossing his arms and sitting back in the chair. "If you aren't totally sure, then make sure you do a little soul searching yourself before you enter into anything with her."

"Thanks, man. I'll be working on that tonight."

"So I guess that is your answer then?"

"Yeah, I think so. I told her I'd have an answer to her by this weekend."

"Well, just be careful. Make sure it's the right thing for you, and if you need anything, just call me, okay?"

Hunter got up and walked to the door, turning the handle, and was just about to leave when I cleared my throat.

"Hunter?"

"Yeah?"

"She wants it to be natural and fun. How the hell am I

going to do that?"

"Treat her no different than the way you've treated the other women you have been with." He shrugged.

"No. I just mean she's my friend. It's going to awkward enough. I don't want to fuck this up."

"Fuck, do you need me to teach you how to use your fucking cock too?" He chuckled. "I dunno, get her some toys, have fun with it. Get her worked up, just relax, and have a good time. Remember, it's only a week, and since there is no relationship going to be formed, you really can't possibly fuck anything up."

That was Hunter's advice. Before I could tell him I was more worried about fucking up my friendship with her, he had already left my office and was on his way.

I stepped out of the shower and wrapped a towel around my waist. I dripped dry while I shaved, and then I walked to the kitchen with a renewed sense of who I was. The weight of having the decision lifted off me had made me feel much lighter than I had in days.

I pulled the fridge open and grabbed a beer and wandered into the living room. Flopping down onto the couch, I turned on the TV to catch some late-night news.

I needed to unwind. The tension I'd been carrying in my upper back and neck all week was now killing me. As I had driven home, I'd been happy with my decision, but now I realized that I wasn't proud of most of the things I had done when it came to women. I let out a breath. I didn't want Sophie to become just another woman on that already long list.

I thought back to the afternoon. All I had gotten from Bryce were wisecracks about my sex life. Hunter had been the one who had made the most sense. He had spoken to me from his heart. He genuinely wanted me to be prepared.

I picked up my cell phone, checking again to see if she had messaged me while I had been in the shower, but the only message that sat there was mine. "Fuck," I mumbled under my breath.

I threw my cell phone down on the couch beside me and reached for the documents I had printed earlier and started reading them over once again, making sure everything I wanted to be included was there. I was about halfway through them when my phone started to vibrate, and when I looked down at my screen, I saw Sophie was calling.

"Moment of truth," I murmured before taking a deep breath. I hesitated for a moment and stared at her name, and then I picked up my phone and answered.

Chapter Nine

Sophie

"I heard from Chase," I practically shouted into the phone. "He said yes." My stomach flopped at the thought. I lay in bed staring up at the ceiling, twirling a strand of my hair around my finger as I waited for a response from Jenna.

"EEEK! All right, girl, this calls for a day of shopping. We need to get your primped and primed and ready. We need to shop. We need to go to the spa and get things waxed. Oh, I am so excited. When is he coming? No pun intended." She laughed.

"Tomorrow, for one week."

"You guys live two blocks away from one another and you're taking him hostage?"

I was giddy with excitement and began laughing. "No. It's part of my plan. I have to maximize my time."

"Maximize your time?"

"Yes, that way we can get in as many sessions as possible."

"You make it sound as if this is a therapy appointment."

I let out a laugh. "I guess you are right."

"Okay, if you say so. Well, this calls for a girls' day, so get dressed. We are going out."

"What? I can't. I have so much to do," I said, looking around my already spotless apartment.

"Yeah, sure, I know you. You are laying there thinking your apartment is such a disaster when in fact you could eat right off your floor because you can't even find a piece of lint. So whatever you need to do, we will do it together. Get ready. I'm coming to pick you up."

Before I could say anything, Jenna was gone, and I threw my phone down on the bed and let out a breath. Twenty minutes had gone by before I had gotten up and showered, and now I sat beside Jenna at Kings Cove's only day spa, Pampered Soul, with my feet propped up on the footrest while some woman went to town filing the soul of my foot.

"What color polish would you like?" she asked me, handing me a color selection to choose from.

I looked over at Jenna, who was rooting through her purse for something and let out a breath. I had just begun flipping through the colors when Jenna suddenly ripped them from my hand.

"Oh no, no, no, no, no, no, you don't. I will choose. You need something hot and sexy. She needs something hot and sexy for her date," she said, smiling at the girl.

"I'm capable of choosing hot and sexy," I said, trying to reach for the color selection and failing as Jenna pulled them farther away from my reach.

"Oh no, the last time you needed to select hot and sexy, you ended up choosing clear coat. No, no, we need something more like this." She held out a deep, dark-red color.

I looked at her as if she had lost her mind. There was no way I could wear a color like that. "Jenna, no way. Bogota Blackberry is not going on my toes."

"Oh yes, it is. She will take this one please," Jenna said, handing the colors back to the pedicurist. "Actually, make it two please. You'll see, clear coat is something my grandmother wears, and she hasn't had a date in years," Jenna said, smiling and looking immensely proud of herself.

"Jenna," I bit out, trying hard not to laugh at the face she was making.

"Girl, you need to chill out. Now sit back, relax, and

don't worry. Just trust me." Jenna sat back and closed her eyes, urging me to do the same.

I finally sat back and did my best to enjoy my time with Jenna. It took an hour, and now we finally sat waiting while our toes dried. Jenna had just put her phone back into her purse and looked to me. "Okay, so what is next?"

"Well, I need to shop for food, wine, flowers, and candles."

She glanced down at her phone and then over at me. "That's all? What about lingerie? Sheets? Perhaps a scented bubble bath? Give me your list." She held out her hand, and I reluctantly placed my folded list in it. She opened the paper and read over what I had written, and without a word, she pulled a pen from her purse.

"What are you doing?" I frowned as she circled some things, crossed others out, and chewed on the end of her pen, lost in thought.

"I'm making some...ah...shall we say, minor adjust-ments. Do you trust me?"

"Ha, yeah, look at my toes. Do I trust you. Clear coat would have been more...me."

"Yeah, and the next thing I know, you will be going to the old-age residence over on Madison and partaking in bingo night. All right, girl, let's go, we have lots to do." Jenna said, dropping my list and the pen into her purse.

Twenty minutes later, we walked through Bed Bath

and Beyond, making our way to the bedding department. I stopped at the first sheet display I came to, the one I always purchased from, while Jenna continued to make her way deeper into the department. I had decided on my usual sheets in a different color and was about to make my way over to the candles when I heard Jenna call my name. I turned around to see her walking towards me holding a package of sheets over her head. I wandered over to meet her, afraid of what she was going to present me with.

"These. These are the best sheets in the world. These are what you need." She shoved the package into my hands and took the sheets I had chosen and threw them on top of the nearest display.

"But I like what I had."

"Sophie, my love, trust me. Matt loves these sheets. They were the sheets I had on my bed the first time we...you know."

I held my hand up to stop her from divulging anything else. I knew I wasn't going to get away with anything different, so I succumbed. "Fine, but I'm taking these too," I said, grabbing the other package.

"But those ones are not going on your bed. These ones are," she said, grinning at me while she shook the package.

"I don't see what it matters, honestly. Sheets are sheets."

"Girl, trust me, it matters!"

"I'm not trying to seduce him. We are having sex for one purpose, that is all."

Jenna burst out laughing. "Girl, there is nothing wrong with a little seduction. This is Chase Malone! You need to have some fun. I'm sure he'd appreciate a little seduction! Plus, the remaining women in this town that have yet to sleep with him would kill for this opportunity. Are you blind? Do you not see them looking at him every-where we go?"

"To be honest, I've never really paid attention. Besides, I wouldn't know how to seduce him anyways." I shrugged and continue following Jenna through the store. Just as we approached the cash register, she stopped and turned to me, grabbing me by the shoulders. "You need to have fun with this, Sophie. Relax and have fun. I know it's a new concept for you."

I ignored her words, made my way to the checkout, and paid for my purchase. As soon as we were out of the store, Jenna was pulling me over to Forever His, a small lingerie store. I walked over to my usual table—cotton bras and panties—and glanced over to where Jenna stood. I could feel my face heating at the items she was sifting through. I stood there blushing just from watching her. It wasn't a wonder I had never made my way over to that table, those things totally intimidated me. Ignoring Jenna, I turned back to the table I was looking at and picked up a couple of pairs of panties when I heard her call my name.

"Oh, Sophie, this would great on you!" She held up a black lacy bra.

I swallowed hard and nodded. I guessed I could pull it off, until she held up the matching panties. "Are they....are they crotchless?" I whispered, ripping them out of her hand before anyone saw what she was holding up.

Jenna let out a loud laugh. "Yes! You need these."

"Jenna, no. There is no way I am going to wear those," I said, turning my back on her and sifting through the pile of cotton panties that were way more my speed.

"Come on, Soph. Come on, lighten up. These are fun!" She giggled, "Matt loves..."

I held up my hand to stop her, "SHHH...I don't even know who I am shopping with right now," I said, throwing down the panties I had picked out and went to walk away.

"It's your best friend, who is making sure you are going to have the time of your life this week." She shoved the bra and panties into my hand, looking me in the eyes. "Trust me. One week, Sophie. One short week, and then you are going to have a bun in the oven, and your sex life will be over."

I burst out laughing. That was the funniest thing I'd ever heard—my sex life. My sex life in the last five years had consisted of two men. That was it. One who never made me orgasm, and one who kissed like a lizard and had never gotten past third base. So if it was my sex life she was truly worried about, I hated to tell her it was already non-existent.

"What's so funny?"

"My sex life, that is what is funny. It's been so long since I've had sex, I'm pretty sure I almost forget how to do it."

"Well, girl, you better figure it out fast because you have picked the one man in this city who hasn't forgotten how to. You'll be in good hands," she said, raising her eyebrows. "Very, very good hands. Now relax. Come on, let's go over there and look some more, but you are getting these." She closed my hand around the black bra and panties and smiled at me, pulling me with her.

I ended up walking out of Forever His with a bag full of lingerie I'd probably never wear, a much lighter pocketbook, but a very happy Jenna. The rest of the afternoon was spent shopping for food, flowers, and candles. Once I had everything that had been on my list, we headed back to my condo.

Jenna stopped the car outside of my condo and put the car into park. "So you're good? You have everything you need?"

"I think so," I said, grabbing the two bags that sat at my feet. "Can you pop the trunk so I can grab the rest of the bags?"

"Sure thing. Remember, if you need me, call."

I nodded, hugged my best friend, and then climbed

out of her car, grabbing the rest of my bags. I smiled and waved and watched as she pulled away from the curb.

It was almost eleven by the time I finally sat down on the couch with my glass of wine. I had spent the rest of the afternoon making sure that everything had been washed, dried, and put away. I even had the new sheets washed, and they were already on the bed. Jenna was right, they were wonderful, I'd thought as I ran my hands over the high thread count sheets.

I flipped the TV on, pulled the blanket off the back of the couch and over my legs, and sipped on my wine. Tomorrow, Chase would be here, and hopefully by this time, we would be deep in one another. I just prayed that I was truly ready for this...and that I wasn't making a huge mistake.

Chapter Ten

Chase

I stared down at the mess of papers in front of me and let out a deep sigh. I had been going over and over them, and I was still unsure if this was how I should proceed. I ran my hands through my already disheveled hair and took a sip of my first cup of coffee of the morning. I flipped on the stereo, and light jazz poured through the speakers. I took another sip of coffee and looked back down at the mess of words that sat in front of me. What would she think when it was time for me to present this agreement to her? Was she going to hate me? Would she be fine with it?

I grouped the papers together, straightened them, and then reread them for the thousandth time. What the fuck had I agreed to do? I thought to myself, and threw the documents down on the table. I sat back and ran my hand over my face.

I drank down the remainder of my coffee and glanced at the clock. I had to get moving if I was going to be on time. I had slept in this morning, like I normally did every Sunday. Today, though, I had brunch planned with my brothers, and I knew they would be waiting for me.

I grabbed the papers off the table, dropped my mug in the kitchen sink, and headed down to my bedroom. An hour later, I was showered, packed, and the kitchen was tidied, and I was on my way out the door to meet the boys for brunch before heading to Sophie's for the week.

I walked into Deb's Place and nodded to our usual waitress before walking into the dining area. Hunter sat over in the corner alone and waved once he saw me.

"Hey, man, where is everyone?" I asked, taking a seat across from him.

"Carter isn't back from his weekend ventures yet, and Mia's brother decided to extend his family's visit. So, it's just us this morning. How you doing?"

Honestly, I felt as if I were going to be sick. The coffee I had this morning kept repeating on me, and my stomach hurt too much for food. I was nervous, afraid I was making a mistake, but I ignored all those feelings and smiled at my brother. "I'm great!"

I signaled to Andrea to fill my cup with coffee. "Bullshit, you're great." Hunter said chuckling, "Is that why you look like you're going to throw up?"

I ran both hands through my hair and looked at my much-older brother, ignoring what he had just said and thinking about what needed to be done before I could go to Sophie's. "I guess I'll feel better once I am at her place and everything is out in the open and done." I shrugged.

Hunter chuckled. "Yeah, once your balls deep in her, eh."

"What can I get for my favorite men this morning?" Natasha asked, stepping up to the side of the table.

"Our usual: poached on toast," Hunter said, handing over the menu.

"Sure thing," she said, taking the menus and winking at me as she walked away.

"So, did you get that paperwork finished?"

I nodded. "Yeah it's done."

"Good." Hunter picked up his coffee cup and took a mouthful.

"Yeah, it is good. There is only one problem."

"What is that?"

"Well, the more I read it, the more worried I'm getting. I just don't want to come across as being an asshole, you know?"

"Dude, what is wrong with you? You are protecting yourself. You're being smart. That's it. Just look at it that way. People get fucking crazy when things go wrong or when they are faced with a situation that they can't handle. You know that, or you should. We all deal with it all the time. I can look it over, if you want, and make sure you haven't missed anything?"

I nodded, drinking down the rest of my coffee just in time for Andrea to come around for refills. "I know they do. It's just I feel that I should be able to trust her."

"You should, but it doesn't mean that you can't put extra precautions in place. Just relax."

My brother was right; there was nothing wrong with a form of protection. It would be something I would suggest to any of my clients. An hour later, fully caffeinated and with full bellies, we stood in the parking lot by our cars while Hunter went over the papers I had drafted. "Good news is everything looks good. I'll witness it once they are signed," he said, handing me the folder. "Where you headed now?" Hunter asked, pulling his car door open.

"The market. I need to pick up a bottle or two of wine and some flowers or something."

"You don't think she has thought of that?"

"I'm sure she has, but I don't want to come off as a total asshole." I laughed. "Just because this is an agreement doesn't mean she doesn't deserve to be treated like a lady."

"All right, man, talk to you later. I have to get home to Autumn and the kids."

I waved as he pulled from his parking spot and

climbed into my car. The market was jammed as I maneuvered myself through the aisle looking for Sophie's favorite bottle of wine. Finally spotting it, I grabbed two bottles and made my way to the front of the store, but not before I stopped at the flower stand and grabbed a dozen red roses and got in line to pay for my purchase. While waiting, I grabbed my phone from my back pocket and typed out a message to Sophie, letting her know I would be there shortly. She responded quickly, giving me a simple thumbs-up emoji, the same as always.

A half hour later, I stood outside her door listening to her bang dishes around in the kitchen. I set my bag down on the ground, took a deep breath, and lifted my hand to knock.

"Coming," I heard her call from inside, and suddenly I felt nervous, my stomach flipping. I ran my hand through my hair, picked up my duffel bag off the floor, and flung it over my shoulder. The door opened, and Sophie stood inside, a nervous look on her face, even though she was doing her best to hide it behind a smile.

"Here, these are for you," I said, holding out the wrapped flowers and a brown bag containing the two bottles of wine.

Her face lit up with a smile as she reached out and took the flowers. "Thank you. I guess you should come in," she said nervously and stepped off to the side to let me in.

I followed her into the familiar apartment and shut the door behind me, while she busied herself in the kitchen putting the flowers in a vase.

"Where should I put my bag?" I called.

"In the bedroom." She smiled, carrying the flowers and setting them on the table.

I made my way down the hall to her bedroom and looked inside. Everything had its place. The bed was made perfectly, not a wrinkle in sight. I stepped inside the door and set my bag on the floor by the bed, which immediately looked out of place in the picture-perfect room. I bent down and pulled the documents from inside the bag, holding them tightly, thinking it might be better to get this over and done with first than to wait until later. I didn't want to get in the moment with her and then decide to spring this on her tomorrow or later in the week.

I pushed my sleeves up and headed back out to the front room to find Sophie sitting on the couch, two glasses of wine in front of her. She patted the spot beside her for me to sit down, but not before she noticed the folder that I carried with me. I blew out a breath and took a seat as I watched the unsure look in her eyes.

I took a sip of wine, set the glass down, and then cleared my throat. "Sophie, listen, before we get started here, I think we need to go over a few things."

Her eyes met mine in question. "Okay," she said hesitantly, unsure of where I might be going with this.

There was no easy way to bring this up, so I set the documents on the table in front of her. "Okay, so don't be angry with me, but I need you to sign these."

"What is it?" she asked, picking the documents up off the table, reading the top page, a frown settling on her face as she glanced at the document. "An NDA? You want me to sign an NDA? Why?"

"It's not only an NDA but also a contract. It just states that I am only responsible for providing you with sperm, that is it. That you won't come after me for things such as child support. It also states that I don't want visitation, and that I won't come after you for custody in the future. The NDA is just to ensure that this...transaction, if you will, will remain solely between us. That it won't get out that I am the father of the baby."

I watched as she read through the documents silently. "Chase, I don't understand." She swallowed hard as she flipped through them again. As I watched her, I could see her cheeks getting flush, and she was breathing rapidly as her eyes began to get glassy. I could tell she was struggling with this, and that was exactly what I didn't want.

I reached out and placed my hand on her arm. "Don't worry. It's just to protect us both." I thought I was going to have to keep explaining, but she reached for the pen that was sitting on the table and quickly scribbled her name on the bottom line of both documents. Then she passed me the pen without making eye contact, and I too signed the agreement.

I set the folder off to the side and picked up the glass of wine that sat in front of me and held it out. "I'd like to propose a toast," I said, waiting for her to pick up her glass. She let out a little huff and looked at me, and with a little shake in her hand, she picked up her glass and held it out towards me.

"Here's to one week. Let's hope my swimmers travel far and everything goes well to give you what you want," I said, clinking my glass against hers. I brought my glass up to my lips and sipped the cool liquid. Instead of drinking from hers, Sophie set the glass down on the table and jumped up off the couch. I watched as she walked across the room without saying anything, and then she stopped and lifted her hand to her eyes before turning around to look at me.

"Can you please excuse me for a moment. I, um, I need a minute." Before I could stop her, she had walked down the hall, leaving me alone in the living.

Chapter Eleven

Sophie

The panic had started way before Chase had even arrived. It had started with shopping and had gotten worse by the time he had knocked on the door. The contract was what had literally sealed the deal. I did everything in my power not to shake as I signed my name on that very solid black line, and I had held it all together perfectly, until he had raised his glass and made that toast. As our glasses clinked together, I knew there was no way I would be able to take a sip of wine.

I had managed to walk away, my chest heavy, tears burning in my eyes. I had gotten out the words in time before that solid lump settled right in the middle of my throat, constricting my voice.

He, of course, agreed, letting me know he would be right there waiting for me when I returned. I practically ran across the plush carpet and into the bathroom, every step of the way fighting back the tears that threatened to fall. I closed the door behind me and leaned up against it, closing my eyes tightly.

I needed somewhere private and quiet, just in case I started to cry. I didn't want Chase to hear me. I didn't want him to know that it was his contract that had upset me. I also didn't want him to know that, right at this moment, I wasn't sure I wanted him to be out there when I returned. I tried to fight back the tears, but before I knew it, a single tear fell from the corner of my right eye, making a path for more to follow. What the hell was I even doing?

I tried to calm myself, but the more I thought about this entire situation, the more upset I became. I stepped in front of the mirror and wiped the tears from my cheeks and looked at my reflection. I was the one who had proposed everything like a business deal. I was the one who had mapped it all out. He was right, this was a transaction, nothing more. A simple exchange, if you will.

What had I really expected him to do? He's a lawyer—a very smart and successful one at that. Of course, he was going to want to protect himself; he would be stupid not to. I would be stupid not to protect myself too, but this was Chase, a man I had known my entire life and one I trusted very much. I didn't think I needed to protect myself against him.

I picked up my pressed powder compact and smoothed some on my skin, trying to get rid of the tear lines. I checked my reflection in the mirror.

Perhaps he was right and a contract would be for the best. Even though Chase was my best friend, I couldn't imagine raising a child with him. The man was a successful lawyer, but his personal life was a complete disaster. With him not wanting to be in the picture, I didn't need to worry about co-parenting. I wouldn't have to worry about someone spending their time undermining what rules I had put into place. Besides, I couldn't even begin to imagine Chase raising a child. I had seen him with his brothers' kids; he was a nightmare.

The last time he had watched Hunter and Autumn's little girls I was called to the rescue because one of them had gotten gum in her hair and he panicked. A little ice and it came right out. I laughed at the memory. I remembered walking in the door and finding Chase with a pair of scissors and a screaming child begging Uncle Chase not to cut her hair. I smiled to myself and the memory, swallowed hard, checked over my makeup, and let out a breath. This was the right choice. He was right.

I ran my brush through my hair and shut the light off.

I made my way back down the hall and walked back out into the living room. Chase was still sitting on the couch in the same place I'd left him. I walked around and sat down beside him, picking up my glass and drinking down my wine. I glanced to Chase, and the more I looked into his trusting blue eyes, the more I felt I needed to drink. I grabbed the bottle I had left on the table and poured myself another full glass, drinking that one down just as fast—if not faster than the first one. The tension in the room was so thick that I was having a hard time breathing.

He watched me as I poured my third glass of wine, emptying the remainder of the bottle into my glass. "Whoa, Soph, slow down," he said, taking my glass from me. "We have all night, sweets." He placed his hand on my thigh, giving me a squeeze.

I smiled at the nickname "sweets," a name he had given me when we were fifteen, and one he had never let go of. I swallowed hard. My eyes burned, and the jumbled ball that sat in the pit of my stomach was making me uncomfortable. I was beyond nervous, and I suddenly wondered how on earth we were going to do this, especially if I felt this way just sitting here beside him fully dressed.

"Everything okay?" he asked. I nodded as he took my hand in his. "So how did you want to go about this?" he whispered.

I thought for a moment. How *did* I want to go about

this? I had no clue. I figured he would have had it all figured out; he was far more experienced than I was in this department. I let out the breath I was holding and shook my head. "I dunno. Perhaps...perhaps, maybe we should kiss first." I shrugged.

"Okay, we can do that."

He stood from the couch and reached for my hands, pulling me to my feet. He pulled me closer to him. The smell of his cologne and the touch of his hand on my waist sent a chill through my body. His hand didn't remain on my waist for long because, as quickly as he touched me, he pulled his hand away as if he had been burned. Instead, he gripped my hand with his and pulled our hands between us. He leaned in, turning his head in the same direction I had turned mine. We were as awkward as we had been the first time he had kissed me, only that time he had succeeded.

"This isn't going to work," I mumbled, frustrated, placing my hand on his broad chest and pushing him away.

"Whoa, whoa, what isn't?"

"All of this...It's pointless. I mean, we can't even share a simple kiss. How are we supposed to sleep together?"

Chase stood there staring at me. I could tell he didn't know what to say, and I didn't blame him. Finally, completely frustrated, I stepped away from Chase and walked over to the window. I looked out over the city and did my best to concentrate on anything else than the problem at hand. I heard Chase clear his throat, and I turned around in time to see Chase pull his phone from his pocket and begin dialing.

"What are you doing?"

"We, Sophie Lancaster, have a date. We are going out. Chase Malone doesn't give up this easily. You of all people should know that," he said as he typed something into his phone.

I looked at him wide-eyed. "Going out? Where are we going?"

"You'll see. Grab your jacket. Let's go," he said, making his way to the door, slipping on his coat and shoes.

We had walked over to Kings Cove Park as the sun began to set. "Where are we going? Are you going to tell me?" I asked again, running to catch up to him for the third time.

"We are going on a horse-drawn carriage ride through the park. I want to just chill a little. I know the guy who runs the carriages, so I messaged him and he said the guy would be waiting for us at the east entrance."

I slowed down and was just about to protest when the east gate came into view, and just as Chase had said, a horse-drawn carriage was already sitting there waiting for us.

"Come on, Soph, pick it up a little," Chase called and

approached the driver, introduced himself, and slipped the man some money.

"Where to, sir?"

Chase looked in both directions before answering. "Through the park down to the water?"

"Sounds good, sir."

Before Chase returned to my side, he leaned in and whispered something into the man's ear. He nodded and turned to smile at me. "Climb in, miss."

Chase stepped up beside me and placed his arm around me, his cologne invading my senses. "Climb in," he whispered, staring into my eyes, taking hold of my hand and helping me up into the carriage.

I had just sat down when he climbed in beside me and reached for one of the blankets that was folded neatly beside me and threw it over our legs just as the carriage pulled away from the sidewalk.

I sat back and breathed deeply, trying to relax as I listened to horses' hooves clapping along the pavement. I watched the birds flit through the trees. As the gentle breeze blew, I closed my eyes and just sat listening to the sounds around me.

"How did you know I've always wanted to do this?" I whispered more to myself than Chase, even though it was directed at him.

"You've never done this before?"

I shook my head. "Never." I looked over to him, and a soft smile sat on his lips.

"I guess you could say it was a lucky guess then." Chase placed his arm behind me and sat back, encouraging me to do the same, finally pulling me against his body.

I finally felt myself starting to relax as I listened once again to the sounds around me. It was almost therapeutic, and once we turned into the tree-lined lane heading towards the water, the thousands of tiny lights the city always put up at this time of year had come on, lighting our way.

I felt Chase kiss the top of my head. "Are you enjoying this?" he whispered.

I nodded and smiled to myself. I closed my eyes and enjoyed the breeze across my face when I felt the carriage finally came to a halt.

"Sir, I believe this is the stop you requested."

I opened my eyes in time to see the driver turn and nod to Chase.

"Thank you. Oh, and there is no need to wait. We can walk back," Chase said, throwing the blanket off us and climbing out of the carriage. He held his hand out for me to take. I let out a little squeal of surprise when he grabbed me around the waist instead and lifted me down.

Once I was on the ground, he grabbed my hand, and

together we walked for a bit, coming to a clearing at the edge of the lake. Chase stopped at the first bench we came to and looked around but then shook his head. "Nope, not this one," he mumbled under his breath as he looked out over the water.

I frowned. "What is it? What are you looking for?" I questioned, but he held his hand up, ignoring me and walking ahead to the next bench, then to the next bench, until finally he stopped and sat down.

"Have a seat," he said, patting the bench beside him and smiling up at me.

I laughed and took a seat, looking out over the calm water. "So what is so special about this exact spot?"

Chase looked at me and put his hand over his heart, acting as if I had fatally wounded him. "Sweets, I'm shocked. You don't remember?"

I shook my head, laughing at his actions. "No, I'm sorry, I don't."

"Come here." He got up off the bench and moved a few steps ahead. When I didn't jump right up, he waved his hand impatiently, signaling for me to join him. "Come on."

I rolled my eyes, let out a breath, and stood, taking a step forward and stopping beside him.

"No, it was more like here," he said more to himself as he grabbed me and positioned me where he wanted me to stand. "What about now?"

"I'm sorry, but I've got nothing." I giggled, shrugging my shoulders.

"Trust me?" he asked as he stepped closer to me yet. I could feel the heat from his body and smell his cologne as he stepped in even closer to me. My heartbeat accelerated, and I let out a breath as Chase stepped up against me, his chest lightly brushing against me.

"Yes," I answered, my voice shaking, swallowing hard.

"Close your eyes," he whispered. I could feel his breath on my cheek as he leaned in and tenderly brushed his lips across mine. My eyes opened instantly, and Chase pulled his head back to watch my reaction. The first thought I had was to pull away, but that thought was soon replaced by curiosity. Instead I leaned in closer toward him, and he bent in again, this time pressing his lips hard into mine. His arms slowly and gently wrapped around my body and pulled me even tighter against him, his tongue brushing against mine.

It didn't take long before I was lost—lost in his kiss, lost in his arms, lost in the moment between us. I heard nothing around us, and I had forgotten everything. When his tongue brushed through my mouth again, I pressed my body harder into him. His hand rested on my cheek as he sucked my bottom lip into his mouth, finally pulling away, leaving my lips feeling empty.

"Open your eyes. Now do you remember?" he whispered.

I opened my eyes and looked into his and gently smiled. In an instant it all came rushing back to me. The old courthouse now turned into the Whisper Wind Restaurant off in the distance behind him. "I do, I so do. This was the place of our very first kiss."

"Hopefully, this one was a little better than that first kiss so long ago." He chuckled and brushed a strand of hair off my face, studied my gaze, and then leaned in and met my lips again.

"A little," I mumbled and met his lips again.

Chase Malone knew how to kiss—gentle yet firm, with just enough tongue, and like everything else he did, he put his whole self into it. I was now afraid of what it would be like to sleep with him if he put that much effort into kissing. I was scared that he would ruin me completely for anyone else.

Chapter Twelve

Chase

I hadn't wanted to stop kissing her. I had wanted to get lost forever in those lips of hers. She tasted so good, and I almost lost it when I heard that gentle moan escape from her as I pulled her body into mine and ran my hands through her long, soft hair. I couldn't remember the last time that a kiss had been so good that I didn't want it to end. I sadly realized that it had to end when I felt Sophie shiver in my arms. The wind had picked up, and I knew I needed to get her back to her apartment, back to warmth and safety and privacy.

A light rain shower had started coming down about a block away from her condo. We had picked up our pace but still got stuck in a sudden downpour that stopped as soon as we hit the front door. We had both taken a hot shower, changed, and now we sat in front of the fireplace on the floor, TV on in the background. A small buffet of Thai food was spread all over the coffee table in front of us.

"Oh my, that was delicious," Sophie said, placing her plate on the table and sitting back against the couch.

"I'm glad you enjoyed." I brushed a strand of hair from her eyes. "How about you find something to watch, and I'll clean up."

"Oh no, that's not necessary. I got it," Sophie said, getting ready to get up, but I took her hand off the plates and shook my head.

"I got it," I said sternly and grabbed our plates while she flipped through the channels and piled some of the takeout containers on top of them and carried them into the kitchen. I cleaned out the leftovers and put them in the fridge. I put the dishes into the dishwasher, and then grabbed one of the chilled bottles of wine from the fridge and two wine glasses. Since we had shared our first kiss, something had changed between us. Not only was I more at ease, but Sophie was as well. The only thing I was worried about now was how she might react if something happened between us tonight.

When I re-entered the living room, Sophie was curled up at the opposite end of the couch from where I normally sat. As soon as I sat down, Sophie grabbed the blanket from the back of the couch and wrapped herself in it, using it almost as a shield.

"Is *The Wedding Singer* okay?" she asked.

"Sure." I shrugged and poured us both a glass of wine, handing her a glass.

"What's with you?" I questioned.

"Nothing." Sophie couldn't fool me; something was bothering her.

"Please, Sophie, I'm not a brand-new guy in your life. Normally, you have your feet in my lap, and you're sprawled out hogging the couch. Instead, you are curled up in the corner hiding under a blanket. What's going on?"

She let out a sigh, looking at me out the side of her eye. "You said you wanted this to happen naturally, but how does that even happen?"

"Believe me, please, it does, but you kind of have to trust me enough to actually touch me, and to let me touch you. It would help if you were being somewhat normal and not worrying your pretty little head. Put your trust in me and fucking relax because you're freaking me out."

Sophie burst out laughing. "I'm sorry." She giggled and threw the blanket off her, sitting up.

"Get over here," I said, holding out her glass of wine and adjusting so that she could sit up against me. She took the wine and edged her way closer.

An hour later things were more normal. Sophie was now curled up at my side, her head resting on my upper abs, her arm wrapped around my waist. My arm was resting around her waist and we lay lazily watching the ending of *The Wedding Singer*.

"You know, I give him props for the public proposal, but how the hell can you take a guy seriously without a ring?"

"What makes a public proposal so special?" I questioned, kissing the top of her head.

"Well, look at him. He is up there risking it all. In front of all those people, he risks the humiliation of her possibly saying no."

"Oh, Sophie, come on. It's totally predictable. I mean, if he thought she would say no, then he would never propose in front of everyone."

"No, I don't agree. I think it totally shows how confident he is and that he fully believes that she will say yes."

"I see. So, do you think that if he proposed in private he wouldn't be risking it all?"

She thought for a second and looked up at me. "I never said that."

"And the ring, what if he forgot it and packed it in his checked luggage?" I shrugged. "You know guys get nervous too and forget things."

Sophie let out a laugh and covered her face, and I took

that opportunity to shimmy my body down a bit to lie beside her.

"That is exactly something you would say," Sophie mumbled behind her hands.

"What is?" I whispered as my one hand softly stroked her hair as the ending credits started to roll. It was silky and soft and smelled good, and I suddenly began to question why we had never decided to be friends with benefits. I mean, sure, she had put an end to my fantasy of dating her quickly when we were young, but we had never explored that aspect of our relationship. She looked up at me and grew serious while I stared into her eyes.

"What are you thinking about?" she mumbled, closing her eyes and resting her head on my chest.

I breathed in her scent and closed my eyes, debating asking her what had been on my mind for the last half an hour. I had run over the words in my mind repeatedly. I cleared my throat. "Why didn't we ever do this sooner?"

"Do what sooner?"

"Why were we never friends with benefits?" My cock instantly jumped at the idea.

Sophie lifted her head and looked me in the eyes and shrugged.

"I've always found you attractive, Sophie. I won't lie, and honestly, I don't think I've ever hid that from you either." I leaned in slowly and allowed my lips to graze over hers, my cock hardening instantly behind my zipper.

"Chase, I know who you are. It's not like it's a state secret. You've been with so many women, and I never wanted to be one of many."

"That makes sense I guess," I said, brushing away the loose strand of hair that had again fallen into her eyes, "but if those are your reasons for why you and I never hooked up, then why did you choose me for this?"

Sophie let out a sigh and rested her hand on my chest and her chin on top of her hand. She was silent for a few moments, and then looked me in the eyes. "This is probably going to sound really stupid, but I know who you are. I also wanted this to be special for me, and I know how you treat women. I've watched you. No matter the state of your relationship, you've never treated one of them badly."

I slowly brought my lips to hers and kissed her softly. It was that moment that I decided I would do whatever it took to make sure that our time together was special for her. When our lips parted and she looked into my eyes, I placed my hand on her cheek and slowly brought my lips to hers again. I gripped her ass with my hand and ground myself into her so she could feel exactly how excited I was for this to begin.

Chapter Thirteen

Sophie

I didn't think I would ever forget the look in his eyes when he placed his hand on my cheek and slowly brought his lips to mine. I would also never forget the first kiss that happened tonight; it was so soft and gentle, how he was nipping at my bottom lip as if he were unsure of himself, unsure of how I would react at my best friend kissing me. He lay beneath me and as we kissed, he gripped my ass, grinding into me so I could feel how hard he was for me. I'd be lying if I said I wasn't hot for him, and if he slipped his hand in my pants, he would see just how true that was.

We now lay side by side, my head resting on his arm as we continued to kiss on the couch. He pulled me into his arms, squeezing part of my body and pulling me closer to him. My hands shook as I shyly began to explore his body. When my fingers touched the button of his jeans, he gripped my hand and placed it on the bulge behind his zipper and he let out a moan as I gripped him through his jeans.

"Let's go," he murmured. He slipped off the couch and, pulling me with him, we wandered down the hall to my bedroom. We hadn't even made it halfway down the hall when he grabbed me and pushed me up against the wall, kissing me hard while his hands roughly explored my body. A shiver ran through me as his hands brushed over my breasts, my nipples already hard and seeking his attention.

He kicked the bedroom door open, grabbed me and kissed me hard as he guided me over to the bed. Our lips parted and we stood before one another, breathless, his eyes trailing from my face down my body. He gripped the edge of my T-shirt and lifted it over my head, dropping it onto the floor. His eyes wandered over my body and suddenly, I remembered I wasn't wearing any of the pretty lingerie I had bought on my shopping trip this afternoon. I had spent a small fortune on all that frilly lace attire, and here I was wearing one of my normal cotton bras and plain old cotton granny panties, as Jenna so appropriately called them.

I started to cover myself up when I was pulled back

into the moment when I heard Chase groan, "You look fucking amazing."

I had no time to react because his mouth crashed hard into mine and his tongue brushed through my mouth, bringing me right back to the moment, and I forgot all about what I was wearing. His hand found my breast, and he brushed his thumb over my nipple as he kissed down the side of my neck. I felt his hands reach around to my back and begin to fiddle with the clasp on my bra when I froze.

"What is it?" he whispered, fighting to take my lips again.

"What if...what if you don't like me?" I questioned. I felt like I was in my teens again. It had been so long since a man had seen me, I was feeling super insecure.

He stopped what he was doing and, still holding me in his arms, looked down into my face. I felt the clasp of my bra go and the material became loose on me. "Impossible," he whispered, smiling at the fact that I hadn't even noticed he had flicked the clasp of my bra.

"You say that...but..."

His lips pressed hard into mine, stopping me from speaking any more than I already had, and he backed me up to the bed. The back of my knees finally met the edge of the mattress, and I fell backward onto my soft bed. He wasted no time. His hands gripped the waistband of my yoga pants, quickly ripping them and my panties off me.

I looked up at him as he stood there between my legs, still fully clothed. I could see his cock painfully straining against the zipper of his jeans as his eyes took in my body. He bent over top of me and took the straps of my bra, the tips of his fingers grazing over my arms as he pulled it away from my body. He kneeled down between my legs onto the bed, one arm supporting the weight of his body, the other hand gently rolling my nipple between his fingers. I moaned into his mouth as his met mine.

"You're beautiful," he murmured as I let out a soft moan as he gently pinched my other nipple between his fingers. He kissed down my neck, pressing tiny kisses along my collarbone, and then running his tongue from my neck down between my breasts. He trailed his tongue up my left breast, rolling his tongue around my nipple, and then sucking it into his mouth. Then he repeated the same action over to the other one. I could feel the heat and throbbing between my legs intensify as he trailed his tongue down my belly, stopping and lightly blowing over my skin.

I felt him slide off the bed onto the floor, and he kissed my lower belly, which caused me to jump. I lifted myself up, resting on my elbows, and watched as he grabbed my legs, placing his hands on the inside of my thighs and forcing my legs open. "You're so fucking wet," he muttered as he blew his warm breath on my already throbbing center.

I watched him as he looked up at me, and I had just about come on the spot listening to his words. I bit my lower lip. He had barely even touched me yet, and my body was already begging for him to make me come undone. I arched my back and bit my bottom lip as he blew over me again. He had me hooked around him, and I felt his hands grip my waist, holding me in place, and then I felt his hot tongue connect with my center, causing my head to fall back in pleasure. His tongue ran through my wet folds once, and I was thriving and panting and fighting from screaming his name as my hands gripped his. The harder I gripped, the harder he gripped back, my body straining as he continued this wonderful torture that was almost too much for me to endure. I couldn't hold back any longer, and I let out a thunderous moan as my release came.

I was completely spent as I rested on the mattress, my eyes closed, trying hard to regain control over my breathing. My heart was beating so hard it felt like it would beat right out of my chest. I lay there in the quietness of my room and heard him chuckle as I felt the bed move, and I opened my eyes to look in his direction. He now stood between my legs. His jeans had fallen to the floor, his hard, thick cock sat in his hand, and his eyes washed over me as he stood there stroking himself.

Before I could say anything, even beg for a moment to regain control over myself, he dropped his cock and gripped my legs, pulling me down to the edge of the bed. He was definitely in control of this situation, and I secretly loved every second of it. Once he had me where he wanted me, he ran his cock through my wet center, placing himself snuggly against my entrance. Bending down, he met my lips as he slowly inched himself inside of me, stretching me, his hands running over me, gripping my body as he pumped deeply into me. I cried out his name and dug my fingers into his back as he pressed his way into me, until he was fully seated in me.

"Soph..." he breathed out as he continued to pump into me, slow and deep. I gripped his back, feeling his tense muscles, his breathing ragged, and thought for a second that I felt his body quiver. He hands gripped my body tightly, stiffening as he poured himself into me. He collapsed against me, catching his breath.

We now lay in the dark, my head resting on Chase's chest, listening to his heart beating. His fingers danced in tiny circles on my shoulder, occasionally kissing the top of my head. "What are you thinking about?" I asked.

"I just don't want you to think that I am always that weak. I can normally go for hours."

I blushed at his words, not sure what to say.

He chuckled a little. "I'm also really curious as to why we waited so fucking long to do this?" he said, pulling me closer to him.

I thought for a minute. I searched my mind to try and

find some reason that actually made sense for me to answer his question. The longer I thought about it, I quickly realized that I could not come up with anything that made sense. I didn't know if it was because he had just totally blown my mind or because part of me had always secretly wanted him. Whatever the reason, I was glad we finally had, and I was looking forward to the rest of the week. I shrugged and, looking off into the distance, I whispered, "Honestly, I don't really know why."

"Well, that calms me a bit. It must have been good if you're actually answering that question with that answer." He chuckled, placing his arm behind his head, pulling me closer.

I lifted my head and kissed his lips. "I really can't think of a way that it could have been any better. Thank you."

Chase chuckled. "Well, I can." He rolled up onto his shoulder and pulled the blankets up over our head and kissed me hard, his hands roaming over me again, leading us both back down that path of no return.

Chapter Fourteen

Chase

I woke to the shower running. Other than that, the apartment was silent, and the sun was starting to rise over the neighboring apartment buildings. I rolled onto my back, put my arm behind my head, and lay there staring at the ceiling, trying not to think of Sophie naked in the shower, but it was proving to be impossible.

I had laid awake long after Sophie had fallen asleep. I lay there watching her, watching the calmness on her face that I so rarely saw from my best friend. The evening had started off somewhat rough but had ended in mind-blowing sex. I loved my best friend, but at times she was so uptight and worried about everything that it drove me crazy. Especially now she was so worried about how things would end up progressing between us that it had pretty much forced me to pick up my game. That was one thing that was different about her than all the others I dated, I rarely had to work at it, which had made me lazy. Images flashed through my mind of her earlier in the evening. The look on her face when I had taken her on the carriage ride down to the lake, then the look in her eyes at the end of our first kiss. I softly smiled to myself thinking about it. The more I had watched her while she slept the more I realized just how beautiful she truly was. Suddenly, the need to place my lips on hers was overwhelming, and I'd had to force myself to roll over to keep from kissing her again.

I'd had no idea where it had come from, but that same need that I had fought off last night while watching her sleep was starting all over again. My cock was starting to ache at the thought of kissing those perfectly bowed lips. I reached under the sheets and gripped the base of my cock, squeezing it, trying to get the throbbing to stop, but it did little good. "Fuck it," I said aloud to myself and got up from the bed.

I was just about to the bathroom door when I heard the shower shut off. A huge surge of disappointment ran through my body, but I decided to go ahead and open the door anyways. We could always just jump right back into that hot shower.

My hand was just about on the door handle when the door was suddenly ripped away from me and a towel-wrapped Sophie came bursting into the room. Her eyes wandered over my naked body, stopping on my hardened cock. Her cheeks flushed and a small smile came to her lips, which quickly vanished when she saw me looking at her. "Good morning," she murmured.

"Good morning. You're up early this morning."

"Every morning. Where were you going?"

I smiled. "Well, since I woke up in a cold empty bed, I thought I would come in and surprise you, maybe have a little fun in the shower," I said, raising my eyebrows at her and tugging at the knot in the front of the towel, trying to pull her closer, or better yet make her lose that towel she was now clutching tightly.

She stepped back out of my reach. "In the shower?" She scrunched up her nose in this cute way I had never seen her do before, or perhaps had never noticed, at my suggestion.

I did my best to suppress the laugh that threatened to erupt at her comment. "Come on, have you seriously never done it in the shower before? Shower sex is fantastic."

She shook her head as her cheeks flushed and her gaze hit the floor in embarrassment. She let out a sigh and walked over to her closet and began sifting through the clothes that hung there.

"Wait, you're serious? You've never done it in the shower?"

"You should get dressed, in case you forgot today is Jenna's birthday. We have plans with her and Matt tonight, and I still need to grab a gift for her."

"Come on, Soph, I didn't mean to upset you." I frowned and watched as Sophie clutched the towel tighter to her body. She ignored me by starting to search through her closet. I hadn't meant to upset her. Hell, I wanted to throw her over my shoulder, take her in that bathroom, and make her forget about anything and everything she felt she needed to do today. I was about to grab her waist and pull her into me when she looked over her shoulder in my direction.

"Didn't you hear me? Are you going to get ready or are you going to stand there all day and stare at me?"

The smile fell from my face when I realized she was serious and I made no further attempts to talk about the subject. Instead, I grabbed my bag that sat on the floor at the bottom of the bed and went into the bathroom, shutting the door behind me.

We had spent most of the afternoon at the mall looking for a gift for Jenna. No matter what I had suggested, Sophie flat out turned it down. I was beginning to get very irritated when she finally decided on a gift basket from one of Jenna's favorite stores and a couple movie passes. As the day had gone on, the tension between us mounted, and Sophie seemed to be more on edge than she had been earlier that morning.

I had been instructed to be ready by five, and I stood looking over my reflection in the hallway mirror fifteen minutes early while I waited on Sophie. I rolled up the sleeves of my shirt and straightened my collar as Sophie came out from the bedroom. "You just about ready?" I questioned, glancing at my watch.

"Are you sure we shouldn't just drive our own separate vehicles?" Sophie asked as she grabbed her shoes from the closet and slipped them onto her feet.

"It's fine. If they ask, which I'm sure they won't, but if they do, I picked you up because your car wouldn't start." I shrugged. "They won't think anything of it because I am closer to you than they are. It would make perfect sense that you called me and not them."

"All right, if you say so, but I think it would just be easier to go separately," she bit out, slipping into her coat.

"Why? I'm just coming back here tonight anyways."

You could cut the tension with a knife as we drove in silence to the restaurant. Sophie sat fiddling with the ribbon on the gift bag, as she looked out the window, completely ignoring me. I knew those two things combined meant she was pissed off with me, but I still tried to calm the situation. "You can put the radio on if you like," I offered, pulling out onto the main road. I'd had all the silence I could handle.

"No, it's okay." Sophie shrugged, not once looking my way. "I have a headache."

"Sure, okay a headache, right," I mumbled under my breath. That comment had gotten me a stern look from Sophie, who went right back to looking out the window when I'd glanced at her.

She had been acting like this all day for absolutely no reason, and I was beyond irritated by her cold shoulder. We had never treated one another this way. I pulled up to the stoplight and turned to watch her. She sat there still twirling that stupid ribbon around her finger, ignoring me as if I weren't even there. "Is everything all right?"

"Yes, of course. Why would you ask that?"

I let out a deep breath and prayed I wasn't starting a major argument with my best friend before heading into a birthday celebration for another one of our friends. "Soph, you've barely looked at me since this morning. So you can say what you want, but I'm not an idiot."

"Let me guess, you've been with enough women to know when one is upset with you." She let out a breath, rolled her eyes, and pointed to the sign coming up on our right to show me that we were almost there. I pulled into the parking lot and into the first spot and cut the engine.

"What exactly is that supposed to mean?"

"Just drop it. We are late. Now are you sure you don't want me to go in first? You know how I always arrive before you. If they ask, I'll just tell them that I parked around back."

I blew out a frustrated breath. "Sophie, it's fine," I said as I unbuckled my belt. This was exactly like Sophie, worried about everything. At this point, I didn't care what Matt or Jenna thought. What I cared about and was more concerned with was what she had meant by that snarky little comment. I took one look at her worried face, rolled my eyes, and took her hand in mine. "They aren't going to think anything of it. Just relax," I said, bringing the back of her hand to my lips and kissing her. "Why are you so worried?"

"I'm not worried about anything," she murmured, hiding her eyes from me. Instead of taking two minutes to talk to me, she grabbed the gift bag and her purse from the floor and got out of the car.

I frowned and followed her lead. By the time I had locked the doors and walked around the car, Sophie was already halfway across the parking lot, so I picked up the pace to catch up to her.

We were barely through the door when I saw Jenna wave from the table in the back. Placing my hand on

Sophie's back, I leaned in to whisper in her ear when she suddenly called out to Jenna and went running into the restaurant, leaving me standing there.

I stared down at the half-eaten piece of apple pie that sat on my plate and ran my fork through the sweet, sticky filling. Sophie and Jenna were now out on the dance floor, while I sat with Matt in the booth. I sipped on my Crown and Coke, while Matt told me about one of the cases he was working on at the firm. I knew he was telling me something important, I could tell from the look on his face, but my mind was on one thing and only one thing— Sophie. I couldn't tear my eyes away as I watched how her hips swayed as she danced. She had me entranced, and I couldn't help but allow my eyes to wander her body.

"Did you hear what I said?" Matt snapped his fingers in front of my face as he waited for a response to whatever question he had apparently asked.

"Huh, what?"

"You feeling okay? You barely ate anything, and you're not paying attention to anything I have said."

"Yeah. I'm sorry. My mind is on other things right now."

"I can see that. Care to talk about it?"

I shook my head and looked over his shoulder at Sophie.

"What the hell are you looking at?" he asked as he turned around and looked in the direction of the girls.

"Nothing, it's nothing. So back to what you were saying," I said, trying to pull his attention back to me, but it did little good. In full view, Sophie and Jenna were both dancing and laughing. My eyes were trained on the curves of her hips as she danced on the dance floor with Jenna. I took another sip of my Crown and Coke, trying to calm the ache in my pants, when I noticed Matt staring at me.

"Sophie, huh?" Matt asked, smiling at me. He had seen me staring at her; there was no hiding it now. I fought internally for a few minutes about spilling everything to Matt.

"Sophie what?" I heard Jenna ask, and I looked up in time to see that both Jenna and Sophie stood beside the table out of breath and with smiles on their faces.

I swallowed hard, thinking fast. "Sophie and I should get going," I said, looking at my watch and downing my drink.

"Already?" Jenna and Sophie cried out at the same time.

"Yeah, I have an early morning tomorrow, and I need to drop Sophie off before I head home," I lied. Sophie met my eyes, and I hoped she could read the want in them. I didn't want to fight with her. I just wanted to pin her up against the wall in her bedroom and have my way with her.

"We can take her," Matt announced.

"Yeah, stay," Jenna urged, wrapping her arm around Sophie. "Dance the night away with me."

Sophie looked at me and bit her bottom lip. "No, it's okay. I'm tired anyways," Sophie said, hugging Jenna and whispering something in her ear at which Jenna nodded and smiled.

As we were on our way out of the restaurant, I stopped and took care of the bill for the four of us. I figured it was the least I could do for bailing early. Sophie had wanted to pay, but I insisted.

We drove back to Sophie's condo in uncomfortable silence again. She still would barely make eye contact with me. We had ridden the elevator in silence and were now standing outside the door to her condo. I leaned up against the wall, watching while she fumbled through her purse for the key. If she knew the thoughts that were running through my mind, she might start looking at me a little nicer. "You planning on talking to me tonight?" I asked quietly so we didn't disturb the other tenants.

She continued rooting through her bag and finally pulled her keys, quickly inserting it into the lock and opening the door. She dropped her purse to the floor, kicked off her shoes, and turned to look my way. "What would you like to talk about? My lack of sexual experience for one?"

"Are you serious?"

"Yes, I'm serious." She turned and marched down the hall toward her bedroom. I followed. There was no way I was going to spend the night fighting with her because she was hung up on the stupid idea that I had been making fun of her this morning.

I walked into the bedroom to see her digging through her top dresser drawer and shoving handfuls of what looked like lingerie into a bag. "I take it you told Matt all about how inexperienced I am. Bet the pair of you had a really good laugh over it too."

"What on earth are you talking about? No, I didn't tell Matt anything. What are you doing?"

"I'm getting rid of all this stuff. All the stuff I bought that I am too inexperienced to wear. Not only that, but I'd feel like an utter ass wearing them for you anyways," she barked, continuing to stuff things into the bag.

I walked over and grabbed her hands, stopping her from shoving yet another handful of lacy and silky things into the bag. "Just stop."

"No, I bought this so you'd like being with me. So, I compared to all the others you've been with. Figured you might as well have something that you like to look at if you had to do this." She held out a black lacy bra and panties, which I took from her and looked at. I couldn't help the smile that sat on my lips. They were hot as hell, and I'd probably kill to see some woman in them, but they sure as hell weren't Sophie.

"What? What is so funny?"

"Crotchless panties, Soph, really?"

I met her eyes, her cheeks flushing from embarrassment, which made her look so sexy. "See, you've seen these before. I'd only ever heard of them." She turned away to hide from me.

I looked down at the bra and panties in my hand and dropped them to the floor. I could tell from behind that Sophie was crying; she wiped at her eyes. I walked over and placed both my hands on her arms. "Sophie, this isn't you. These things aren't you."

"What isn't?"

"All this stuff you bought. This isn't you. Guys want to be with the real you, inexperienced or not."

"Well, believe me, I am as unexperienced as they come. You hit the jackpot with that, and if you think different, you're fooling yourself."

"Look, I'm sorry, okay, for however you took my comment, but it wasn't meant to be insulting to you. I also didn't think you would take it the way you did. I don't really care how experienced or inexperienced you are. That's all part of the fun, if you know what I mean," I said, grabbing her and pulling her into me.

Sophie let out a loud laugh and pushed me away. "Sure

it is," she said, ripping the undergarments that I still held in my hand and shoved them deep into the bag. "I must have been a damn fool buying all these. I'm sure you got a kick out of this. Glad I didn't put them on and parade around for you. You probably would have died with laughter."

I grabbed the bag from her hand and threw it over on the bed. "That's enough. That shit in that bag isn't you, and it never will be you, no matter if you'd been with two or twenty men. I've apologized and I meant it. Forgive me or don't."

Sophie stood across from me, not knowing what to say. I wasn't kidding, I wasn't joking. I was done if this was how she was going to act. Within seconds she went from staring at me, wondering if I were being truthful, to being wrapped in my arms, kissing me hard. It had caught me by surprise, but with little hesitation, I wrapped my arms under her ass and lifted her as she wrapped her legs around my waist, and I carried her over to the bed.

Chapter Fifteen

Sophie

I woke with a start, my breathing heavy. The room was dark, and I rolled over to see the other side of the bed was empty. I ran my hand over the sheets, but they were already cold, letting me know that Chase had been up for a while. I rolled over and stretched, my body aching in places I hadn't thought possible. My body relaxed into the mattress, and I thought back to last night.

After we had talked and cleared the air, and made up, we'd decided to catch a movie before bed. I'd changed while Chase made popcorn and found something on. When I walked into the living room, I was surprised to find a blanket sprawled out onto the floor in front of the

TV, pillows thrown down and the fireplace on. I'd frowned at the mess on the floor and was about to ask what was going on when I heard the clink of two glasses. I turned to find a shirtless Chase standing holding two glasses and a bottle of wine.

"Thought we could curl up on the floor, watch a little TV," he said, setting the glasses down on the table and opening the bottle of wine. "Sound okay?"

"Sure, what did you want to watch?" I questioned, grabbing the remote and flipping through the channels. Before I had gotten far, Chase slipped the remote from my hand and replaced it with my wine glass and put the remote onto the dining room table.

"Come, sit down."

I looked at him questioningly but did as he asked anyways and relaxed back into the pile of pillows. Chase grabbed the blanket that sat on the back of the couch and spread it out over top of us, then he, too, sat back and relaxed. "We will watch this," he said, nodding to the TV.

I looked at the screen and giggled. "It's not even in English, and it has no subtitles. How on earth are we going to understand it?"

Chase shrugged and lay down beside me. "Well, the remote is over on the table, so I guess we will have to make do."

"You are crazy," I said, kicking the blanket off me

before trying to stand up, but Chase grabbed my arm stopping me and pulled me down beside him.

"Perhaps, perhaps not." He leaned in and kissed me.

An hour later, we both lay on our sides, Chase spooned up against me as we continued to watch this foreign film. I was about to ask him a question and jumped as I felt Chase grind into me. The ridge in his pants proved that he wasn't paying attention to the movie and wouldn't be able to answer what I was going to ask because he clearly only had one thing on his mind. His lips moved against the back of my neck, kissing me.

"Fuck, I want you," he murmured between kisses as he ground himself into me again. He sucked my earlobe into his mouth before rolling me over and attacking my lips. His kiss felt different this time. It was deeper and slower. His hands moved over my body, and his touch was different as well. It wasn't as firm and cold; instead it was softer, gentler, almost like a caress. When he pulled away from my lips and looked into my eyes, even his look was different. It was as if he were looking into my soul. I closed my eyes, kissing him back.

I remembered last night, how we had gone from making out to having sex on the floor in front of the fire. Afterwards, he had carried me back to the bedroom where we had made love until the wee hours of the morning. It had been the most perfect night, I thought to myself as I lie in the warmth of my blankets, but then reality kicked in, and I looked around the bedroom.

"Sophie, you are imagining things," I said aloud to myself. We hadn't made love. *After all, you have to be in love to make it, don't you?*

I thought back to his tender touch and kiss and how he slowly drove himself into me, and I squeezed my legs together, my center throbbing and driving me crazy. I tried to chase the thoughts of last night through my mind, but it did little good. I closed my eyes and dipped my fingers between my legs, running them through my soaked center, my other hand traveling up to my bare breast, pinching, and rolling my nipple between my fingers. I could feel my orgasm building, and I tipped my head back.

"There is always something so fucking sexy about watching a woman get herself off."

I jumped at the deep voice and pulled the blanket up around my neck and glanced toward the door of my bedroom. Chase stood there leaning against the doorway. He was dressed in light-colored jeans and a white T-shirt that hugged his muscles. He held a glass of juice in one hand and a small pink bag in the other.

"I...oh my God..." I sank down and pulled the blankets over my head. If I had ever wanted to die, now was the time. Not only had he been watching me, but the images going through my mind were of him.

I heard Chase start to chuckle, and then felt the side of

the bed dip down and hands prying the covers off my head.

"I didn't think you were here," I mumbled, still trying to hide my face.

"Well, I wasn't, but I certainly am now."

"Yeah I see that. My God. I want to die. I am so embarrassed."

"Fuck, I'm not. That was damn hot."

My heart was pounding in my chest so hard I was sure Chase could hear it. I was also glad I was lying down because I thought I might pass out. Trying to calm myself down, I then heard the rustle of that little bag he had been holding.

"Which leads me to this," he stated, his voice deep.

I opened my eyes and watched as Chase pulled a little box out of that pink bag and opened it.

"What is that?"

"Just a little something I picked up for you." He smiled and held up a small pink object.

I could feel my cheeks heating as he held it out for me to take. "Take it," he urged.

I shook my head, but he pulled my hand forward and set it in my palm. "What is it?"

"It's a vibrator."

"This is a vibrator?"

"Yes, you wear it on your finger and press it against your clit."

I rolled it around in my hand, the heat in my cheeks still present as he watched me. I didn't know what to say or do for that matter. Did he want me to try it now, when I was alone, or while we were having sex?

"Did you want to try it?" he asked, placing his finger under my chin and lifting my head so I could meet his eyes.

I instantly shook my head no. I'd had enough embarrassment for one day. I couldn't possibly let him watch any more.

"Why not?"

I shrugged. Instead of waiting for me to take the lead, he slipped his hand into mine and flicked the vibrator on. It tickled the palm of my hand. I sat there looking down at this little toy when he took my hand in his. "You're curious, I can tell." He gripped my hand and pulled my hand down between my legs. "Lay back. Let's have some fun," he whispered.

Chapter Sixteen

Chase

I was furious and swore under my breath as I walked down the hall towards my office. I threw the file I'd been holding down on my desk and shut the door. As soon as I was behind my computer, I began typing notes into the electronic client file. How the hell I had allowed myself to be pulled away from Sophie for this type of shit was beyond me.

Sophie and I had spent the morning in bed together. I was absolutely fascinated watching her come undone while playing with that little pink vibrator I had gotten her. I was content and happy, until my phone had rung. I'd ignored the first call, quickly distracting Sophie to focus back on herself. However, when the phone rang for the second and then third time, she huffed out loud and told me just to answer it.

I feverishly typed my notes, completely pissed off that what my client had considered an emergency was nothing that couldn't have waited until Monday. Not that my clients weren't important, but this was something that I could have easily handled over the phone in about twenty minutes and did not require a face-to-face meeting.

"Well, well, look who it is," I heard from the doorway and looked up to see Hunter standing there.

"Hey, man."

"What's got you in here?" he asked, sitting down across from me.

"Apparently, a non-emergency, emergency." I let out a laugh, completing my notes and closing my laptop.

"I see. How's it going with Sophie?"

"Good, I guess." I shrugged. I wasn't really sure how I was supposed to answer that question. After all, my only job was to get her pregnant.

"Good, you guess?"

"Yeah, I mean, it isn't that hard to have sex all the time and get someone pregnant is it?" I chuckled.

"True."

"Listen, I really can't stay and talk. It's Friday night, and I promised Sophie I would bring pizza back with me.

Which it's nearing seven already," I said, glancing down at my watch, picking up the client file and filing it away.

"All right, well, I guess I will see you Sunday night for dinner?"

Good thing I was facing away from Hunter because the mention of Sunday night family dinner had me closing my eyes. I'd totally forgotten because I had promised that I would spend the remainder of the weekend with Sophie and return home Sunday night. It was two more days than we had originally agreed to, but not only did I want to make sure that I had given myself optimal chances of fulfilling my end of the agreement, I didn't really want to leave her.

"You can always bring her along, you know. It's probably just going to be the four of us. Carter and Hope are taking the girls to a dance competition, and Bryce and Mia are up at the cottage."

"I'll think about it, okay." I grabbed my coat off the back of my chair, said good night to Hunter, and made my way down to the lobby.

I walked out the front of the building and to the car. Before I pulled away, I called and ordered the pizza. As I drove down the street, I thought about what Hunter had asked. I had spent the entire week with Sophie, much of the time in her bed, and truth was, I was sad that our time together was coming to an end. I couldn't seem to get enough of her. The little time that we had spent apart today had me missing her more than I really should have, for just being friends. Truthfully, my concentration on the issue at hand had been horrible—not because I didn't consider the clients concerns that this wasn't really an emergency, but because Sophie was the only thing that was on my mind. I was so eager to get back to her condo and to her, that I ran two red lights on my way to the pizza place and another two on the way back to the condo.

I stood in the elevator, pizza box in hand, counting the floors as the elevator climbed. It felt like forever until I hit my stop. The smell of pizza nearly drove me crazy as I made my way down the hall, slid the key in the lock, and walked in. "Hey, I'm back. I got the pizza."

"Perfect, you remembered. I'll grab the plates. I'm starving," she said, popping her head around the corner and smiling. "Oh, and I won't kill you with wine tonight. I grabbed a bottle of Coke when I was at the grocery store this afternoon." She smiled.

"Awesome!" I yelled out, dropping the pizza box on the small dining room table. I opened the lid as Sophie set the plates and bottle of Coke on the table.

"Half extra cheese, half double pepperoni and cheese." I smiled as I looked down at the steaming pie, my stomach letting out a loud grumble.

"Chase, seriously, you taint my extra cheese with the taste of your pepperoni?"

"You certainly haven't complained about my

pepperoni all week," I said, smiling. When she didn't laugh, I bumped her arm. "Come on, I have suffered through wine with pizza for you. The least you can do is suffer through pepperoni." I chuckled, pulling her in closer. She rolled her eyes and grabbed a slice from the box.

"So is Friday night always pizza night?" I questioned, grabbing two slices and joining Sophie on the couch.

She nodded as she bit into her slice. "I count it as my one and only treat during the week. Something I can look forward to and not feel guilty about."

"And you're really serious about pepperoni? Seriously, it's so good. You really should try it. Live a little," I said, laughing as I took a bite.

With her mouth full, she shook her head and smiled. "Uh-huh."

She was adorably cute as she sat there shoving food in her face. "What is it about it? I really couldn't imagine ever having pizza without it."

"It's the taste. The whole entire pizza ends up tasting like it. Not to mention the pool of grease that sits in your stomach afterward, along with all the extra calories that I don't need added to an already high-calorie meal."

"So, are you telling me you won't kiss me tonight because of pepperoni?" I leaned forward, blowing kisses her way. She shoved me away as she laughed out loud.

"I never said that."

"Well, that's a good thing, because I don't know how the hell I would help you work off all those extra calories you just consumed if you won't kiss me." I winked at her, leaned in, and met her lips.

Once I was finished, I set my plate on the small table in front of us and leaned back, kicking my feet up on the coffee table. I dropped my head back and closed my eyes for a moment, then I looked over to Sophie to see her face had grown serious.

"Is something wrong?"

Sophie shook her head and cleared her throat. "I have something I want to ask you," she bit out.

"Okay."

I studied her face as the difficulty of whatever it was that she was going to ask etched over it. "Don't feel pressured to say it's okay. If you are pissed off and upset with me, just tell me okay."

I frowned. I had no clue what she was talking about. I had literally left her in bed naked, writhing from a third orgasm this morning, when that call had come in, and I had spent the afternoon at the office. "Sophie, what is it?"

"Before all this started, before I had signed the agreement and the NDA, I sort of told Jenna about this. It's been eating at me since the other night. That was why I was so stuck on taking our own vehicles and why I was somewhat upset when we had gotten home."

I tipped my head back and closed my eyes tightly as

she spoke. It certainly wasn't what I wanted to hear, to know that someone knew what was going on between us.

"I'm sorry. I needed her help to shop and things. I was so nervous, and I never really thought that you would make me sign anything, but now I'm afraid that if you were to find out any other way, you'll be even more pissed off with me than you probably are right now. Please, Chase, don't hate me."

I sat there with my eyes closed trying to contemplate why I wasn't severely pissed off with her at this moment. I wasn't angry that her best friend knew. I also wasn't pissed that Matt probably knew too. I was shocked that with that revelation there was still nothing more that I wanted to do than to still be here with her. I let out the breath I was holding and looked over to her. She sat there, completely unsure of herself, biting on her thumb as I considered what I should tell her. When I saw the tear leave her eye, I quickly decided I needed to say something to her to calm her nerves.

I sat forward and placed my hand on her knee. "It's okay. Don't worry about it. I am sure that the information isn't going to go anywhere." I shrugged.

"So you aren't going to sue me?"

I let out a loud laugh. "No, Sophie, I'm not. However, you are going to owe me."

Her eyes lit up with surprise, catching me off guard. "What...what do you want?" she asked, biting her lower lip. "I have a little bit of money in investments. You can have that."

I let out a laugh at her suggestion. "I don't want money." I laughed. "Instead, I'd like it if you join me Sunday night."

"What for?"

"Sunday night is family dinner night. You, my dear, are going to join me."

She let out a laugh as she shook her head. "I don't think so, Chase."

"You don't think so?"

She shook her head. "I don't want to give your brothers the wrong idea."

"The wrong idea? Hell. But it's okay you told Jenna?"

She thought for a few moments, every once in a while glancing at me. "Okay, you might be able to sway me."

"What might you want?" I questioned, studying the playful look in her eyes.

She didn't say anything. Instead, she got up off the couch, turned the TV off, peeled off her shirt, throwing it to the floor, and started walking down the hall to the bedroom, stopping to turn and look back at me as she reached behind her and unclasped her bra. Instantly, my cock hardened and I reached for the lamp, shutting it off, and ran down the hall after her.

Chapter Seventeen

Sophie

I trailed behind Chase as he climbed up the front steps of Hunter's home and rang the bell. We heard a loud commotion inside, and then the door opened and Kaylee and Paige came bounding out the front door. They grabbed Chase by the legs, hugging him. I couldn't help but laugh at the excitement in their faces as they hugged their uncle. My heart warmed as he bent down and wrapped his arms around them both, tickling them. They squealed with laughter, and once he had let them go, they both looked up at me.

"Who's that, Uncle Chase?"

"This, girls, is my friend Sophie. Do you remember her? She came and helped me get the gum out of your hair?" Both of the girls laughed and laughed, and then they went running into the house calling out that we had arrived.

"Come on, in you go," Chase said, as he walked down the stairs, placed his hand on my lower back, and guided me in.

"Hey, Chase," Autumn called and came over to greet us. On her hip she carried the newest addition to the family.

Chase leaned in for a hug, kissing her on the cheek. "How is Jessica feeling?" he asked, leaning down, and kissing the forehead of the baby she was carrying.

"A little better. No fever today," she said, brushing the baby's hair off her forehead.

"That's good."

"You must be Sophie," she greeted me with a smile, and then looked between Chase and me. "Would you mind holding Jessica while I get dinner on the table?"

"Oh no, I'm completely—" I couldn't even get the words out of my mouth before Jessica was plopped into my arms. I looked to Chase and then to the baby, and then to the back of Autumn who was already disappearing into the kitchen.

"Chase, I—I don't know...Here, you take her," I begged, holding Jessica out to him.

"No way. It will be good practice for you. You've got this." He grinned.

I could feel the panic starting to climb inside of me when we heard a booming hello from behind us. I turned in time to see Hunter come around the corner and shake hands with his brother. They exchanged a few words, while I stood paralyzed looking down at Jessica.

"Hey, Sophie, how you doing?" Hunter asked.

"I'm good, and you?"

"Good. Sorry, it's pretty crazy around here today. Are you ready to eat? Autumn has been cooking all day."

"Starved," I said, repositioning a wiggling Jessica in my arms just in time for her to throw up right down the front of my shirt.

"Oh, God, so sorry about that," Hunter said, stepping in and taking her from me as I fought back puking myself.

Autumn came out of the kitchen carrying two bowls and took one look at me. "Oh, dear...come with me. I will get you another shirt." Autumn set the bowls down on the table and signaled for me to follow her as she started climbing the stairs.

Chase smiled at me and nodded as I followed Autumn upstairs. By the time I had gotten to the top of the landing, she had already found me a T-shirt, grabbed a towel from the hall closet, and showed me to the washroom. "Come on down when you are ready. I am so sorry about that. She has been feeling unwell for a few days."

"It's okay, no worries."

Autumn smiled at me and went back downstairs. I walked into the washroom and shut the door behind me and turned to look at myself in the mirror. My hands shook as I undid the buttons of my blouse. I ran the cloth under the water and cleaned my chest, then I filled the sink with warm water and soaked the blouse, working at the spot to get it clean. I slipped the T-shirt Autumn had loaned me on, rang the blouse out, and looked at my reflection in the mirror.

Who the hell was I kidding? I had no clue what the hell I was going to do with a baby. I was completely uncomfortable even holding her, and if I couldn't even hold a baby, what the hell was I going to do with my own. I slammed my hands down on the counter and without warning the tears began to fall. I closed my eyes, and for the first time ever I began silently praying that I didn't end up getting pregnant.

A knock on the door startled me. I swallowed hard and turned the tap on, filling my hand with water and taking a sip. "Be out in a minute," I called, wiping the tears from my cheeks.

"Sophie, it's just me. Everything okay?" Chase called out. "You've been up here a while. Everyone was getting concerned."

I took a deep breath and opened the door. Chase

stood there, smiling, looking sexy as hell. As soon as he took a look at me and saw I'd been crying, the smile disappeared from his face. "What is wrong?"

He pushed me back and stepped into the bathroom, shutting the door behind him to give us privacy. As soon as he turned back to face me, I lunged forward, wrapping my arms around him and burying my face in his neck.

"Hey...hey...what is it?" he soothed as he wrapped his arms around me and pulled me against him, trying his best to comfort me.

I couldn't answer him. My throat was tight, and all I could do was cry. I cried because, no matter what anyone said, I was going to miss having Chase around the house. I was going to miss our nights together, our days together. I couldn't truthfully say I'd miss him because he was my best friend and he would always play a strong part in my life. I was more upset with myself, that I had allowed my feelings to take hold, and that in some strange way, I had fallen for him, and somewhere in those few minutes that I had held that baby, the realization came to me: I had decided to have a baby and deny that baby his father. Even though he said he wanted no part of it, I still didn't feel that it was fair. Regardless, Chase held me while I cried, and when I finally pulled away, he looked down into my eyes.

"Are you okay?"

"I will be. Sorry, I guess I was just feeling a little panicked. I was embarrassed," I lied.

"Hey, no problem. I get it. Hunter and Autumn get it. But I came up to tell you dinner is ready. So come on. You can leave your blouse soaking and come up and get it afterward."

"No, no, it's okay. I will just fold it up and ask Autumn for a bag. You'll have to return her shirt to her."

"No worries. Come on." He waited until I folded my wet blouse, took my hand, and together we walked downstairs.

We drove back from Hunter and Autumn's in silence. We had enjoyed a great meal and talked for hours afterward, ending the evening with a game of cards. Chase pulled into the parking lot and cut the engine. He climbed out of the car and came around to open my door.

"Come, I'll walk you to the door," he said, holding his hand out for me to take. We walked hand in hand, and when we stopped outside the main door, I leaned in and kissed his cheek.

As soon as I backed away, he quickly stepped in and met my lips, kissing me hard. He was supposed to be going home tonight, but instead it only took me a few moments before I invited him up for a good-bye drink. As soon as the elevator opened on my floor, I found myself pressed up against the wall and Chase pressed into me. With his hands in my hair, his lips on mine, I eventually guided him down the hall and into my condo. The minute the door was shut, he took over, pulling my shirt over my head, picking me up, and wrapping my legs around his waist and carrying me to the bedroom.

I lay on my left side staring out at the lights of the city. We had made love long into the wee hours of the morning. I still hadn't slept—I couldn't—and I glanced at the clock to see that it was almost five. I would have to get up soon.

Chase lay beside me snoring gently, his one arm under my neck, his other resting gently across my waist. I hadn't been able to stop thinking about the feel of his hands as they caressed my body, or the way he gripped me tighter as he sank himself deeply into me. I couldn't forget the way he looked at me, the words he had whispered or the way he called my name as his muscles tightened, for the first time, as he came.

I smiled to myself at the memory and laced my fingers between his, bringing his hand up to my lips, kissing him. He stirred and pulled me closer to him. "What is it? Everything okay?" he whispered, placing a kiss on my bare shoulder, pulling me back tighter against him.

"Yes. Go back to sleep," I whispered, snuggling against

him. Within seconds, he was breathing against my shoulder, lightly snoring again. As soon as I said those words, it hit me like a train.

In a few short hours, we would be over. Even though I knew the single Chase, I also knew that no matter what type of relationship he was in at the time, he was totally committed. I started wondering what it would be like to be with him like this forever. Every night coming home after a long day and curling against him. I couldn't help but watch him with his nieces tonight, how much they loved him, and how much he loved them. He had gotten down on the floor with them after dinner and allowed them to crawl all over him until Hunter had finally called them off.

I wondered what he would be like as a father, wondered if he would change and be like his brothers if someone really caught his eye. I let out a deep breath. There was no point in wishing it were me who caught his eye because it would never become reality. We had made the agreement. There was no going back on it now.

In the morning, Chase would be gone and our lives would return to normal. He would go back home, back to his single life, and to the women who waited for him. I would go back to tax returns and boring dates, and perhaps in nine months the pitter-patter of tiny feet. I had no right to be sad; this was what I had wanted. Yet when I closed my eyes, I had to fight all the thoughts out of my mind and try to get at least a half hour of sleep before I had to get up and start my day.

Chapter Eighteen

Chase

It had been six weeks since I had left Sophie's. Life had returned to a new normal for me. I sat in my office, files sprawled all over my desktop. I was trying to work my way through the pile before I left for the afternoon. I had been busy and had spent the better part of the last few weeks in client meetings. I had been in contract negotiations with two clients who seemed to take joy in not being able to agree on anything.

"Fuck," I said out loud with a huff as I slapped the file down on my desk, hung up my phone, and checked my watch. I'd have loved to blame my clients for all of my stress, but that wouldn't have been fair because they weren't the reason I was stressing. As a matter of fact, I should be thanking them because they had kept me busy enough to keep my mind off the true stressor: Sophie. I had been thankful at first, but now it seemed both were getting on my nerves.

I got up and shut the door to my office. It was loud in the hall, and I was just about to make a call to my three o'clock appointment to reschedule, since I still didn't have all of the information from them that I had requested. I had just begun to dial when someone knocked on my door.

"Come in," I called, sitting the phone back into the cradle.

"Hey, man. How are things?" Hunter asked as he sat down across from me.

"They're fine, I guess," I answered, letting out an irritated huff.

"What's wrong? Is it the case you're working on?" he asked, spinning the file around and taking a look.

"That and a few other things. I swear these clients just revel in agreeing to disagree, and the other ones haven't provided me with all the information I asked for over a week ago."

"Come on, you aren't new. You know what people are like. If everyone agreed, we wouldn't have a job. As for the information, just keep billing them for every hour that they waste. They will eventually get tired of paying your fee and get you what you need. However, I don't think that is the only thing that is bothering you." He spun the file back around and sat back in his chair.

"It's not."

"Well, what is it?"

I let out a breath and put my hands behind my head. "How long does it normally take to find out if you're pregnant?"

Hunter let out a laugh. "It's not something you should be worrying about, Chase. You won't ever be pregnant."

I looked at Hunter as he continued to laugh at his own poor excuse of a joke. "You know what I mean. Shouldn't Sophie know by now? I mean her medical appointment was this morning, and it's been almost four weeks."

"She might know, she may not. Have you asked her?"

I shook my head, running my hand over my face. "No."

"Well, instead of sitting here torturing yourself, you should try that. In my experience, that is the best way to get an answer. What are you doing for lunch?"

"I already ate. I ordered in."

"All right, man, I'll talk with you later. Call her, ask her, and put an end to your suffering."

"Yep, I'm calling," I said, picking up the phone.

Hunter waved at me and shut the door behind him, leaving me with a quiet office and my own thoughts. I dialed her cell phone and sat there listening to it ring. "Come on, pick up," I whispered. I jumped when I heard her voice, but the excitement eased when I realized it was her voice mail requesting that I leave a message and she would return my call within a day. I threw my cell phone down on the desk and ran my hand over my face. Fuck, I couldn't wait a day. I dialed her home line instead, only to arrive to the same conclusion—a damn voice mail.

I let out a huff, picked up my coffee cup, and made my way down the hall to the employee lounge. A fresh pot of coffee had just finished brewing, thanks to my wonderful assistant, and I poured myself a fresh cup.

"Hey, Chase. How have you been?" I heard a familiar voice ask.

I turned in time to see Chelsea walk into the lounge and sit down at the table. Chelsea and I had dated once or twice over the past year—nothing serious, just a fun romp or two when we were both lonely. Not one of my wisest moves, since we had a rule at our firm that we didn't mix business with pleasure.

"Good, thanks. Yourself?"

"I'm good. Listen, Chase, I have a family event to go to in a couple of weeks. I just broke up with my boyfriend. My mom and dad are expecting a plus one, and I was wondering if you would be interested in accompanying me? I promise I will make it worth your while."

I turned and met her eyes, but the only person who ran through my mind was Sophie. "Um, I, ah... I can't. I have a prior engagement," I lied.

"But you don't even know what weekend it is," she laughed.

"I said I am busy." I picked up my coffee cup, pushed by her, and left the room, walking back to my office.

I walked into my office to find my cell phone vibrating on my desk. I set the mug down and picked up the phone. I saw a message from Sophie was waiting for me. She had texted to tell me that she was just now getting to the doctor. I'd gotten the appointment time wrong.

I blew out a breath and instantly the need to know calmed. I was just about to text her back when reception buzzed my office to let me know my next appointment was waiting for me. I dropped my phone and left my office to go meet my clients. Sophie would have to wait, and this would help me pass enough time to hopefully keep my mind off the news.

Soon one appointment turned into two, and the next thing I knew, it was almost six. I had shut off my laptop and grabbed my cell and checked the last messages exchanged between Sophie and me. It was still the same: she hadn't said anything more, but I was sure she should know by now.

I grabbed my jacket from the back of the door, shut the lights off, and made my way down to the parking lot. I pulled out of the parking lot, my wheels spinning, and began the drive across town to Sophie's office.

Chapter Nineteen

Sophie

It was a little after four-thirty, and I sat in the waiting room flipping through one of the parenting magazines that sat on the table. I was still waiting for the doctor to call me in for my results. I glanced at the clock. I was glad that I had canceled my appointments for this afternoon. This was taking far longer than I had originally thought it would.

I shifted in my seat, trying to get comfortable again. I picked up my cell phone, glancing at the messages Chase and I had exchanged, trying to figure out what I could say to him to ease his mind.

"Sophie," I heard my name being called and looked up

to see the same nurse who had taken my blood work earlier standing waiting for me.

I smiled. I could barely contain my excitement. I already knew that the answer was going to be yes. I could feel it. My period was two weeks late, I was bloated, and call me crazy, but I could already feel the life of my unborn baby boy or girl living inside of me. I hadn't told Chase, but I'd taken a drugstore pregnancy test and gotten a positive result and figured I should see the doctor just to be sure. I quickly folded the magazine and placed my cell phone in my purse, zipping it closed.

I followed her as she led me down the hall. I stopped abruptly when she stopped outside of one of the exam rooms and opened the door. "Just have a seat. The doctor will be with you shortly."

"Thank you." I walked in and took a seat, once again pulling out my cell phone to figure out what to message to Chase. I read over his last few messages and was just about to let him know I would call him as soon as I got home when the door flew open and the doctor came flying into the room.

She smiled and took a seat across from me, quickly signing into the computer. "Sorry to keep you so long, Sophie. The lab was behind. It's been a crazy day here today," she said, blowing out a breath and typing yet another password into the computer.

"It's not a problem, really. I booked this appointment

more as a formality than anything. I'm pretty sure I already know the answer anyways."

"You do?" she said, looking over at me. "Well, why don't you tell me then, and we will see if the power of intuition is right," she said, leaning forward and placing her arms on her knees.

I smiled. "Well, my period is a week late. I am so bloated and tired all the time. I finally broke down and took one of those drugstore tests and it came back positive. I mean, I didn't really need to because I already know I am pregnant. I can already feel him or her inside of me," I said smiling, resting my hand on my belly.

"I see. Well, I always tell my patients that those tests at the drugstore aren't always accurate, and that is why I suggest popping in for a visit too. I am glad to see you took my advice." She sat back and flipped across a couple of screens, reading over what I guessed were my test results. She looked over to me and back to the screen before saying anything.

"Yes, I'll agree with you, all the symptoms line up, so I wasn't really surprised when I got a positive response on the test."

I smiled.

"Sophie, hon, I'm afraid your test results have come back negative."

The room spun as her words hit me like a punch to

the stomach. "That's...that's impossible. I mean, I have symptoms. I have all the symptoms."

"Sophie, you have symptoms of many things, not just pregnancy. You said on the intake form you have been feeling very stressed, your diet has been off, and you haven't been sleeping well. Those three things right there will make your period late."

"No." I sat there biting my bottom lip. "No, are you sure you have the right results? Dammit." I closed my eyes tightly, trying to fight off tears.

"Sophie. It's okay to be upset." She placed her hand on my knee.

"Dammit, just tell me, are you sure?"

She nodded. "Yes, Sophie, I'm sorry. There is no baby." She was silent for a couple of minutes. "You know, sometimes, when we want something so bad that we—"

I held out my hand up to stop her. I didn't want to hear any more. "Well, then, I guess there is no reason for me to take up..." I swallowed hard. "Any more of your time." I grabbed my coat and purse and was just about to head out the door when my eyes began blurring and my head began throbbing. I stopped and pinched the bridge of my nose.

"Sophie."

I inhaled deeply, turning and looking towards her, nodding through tear-filled eyes, and took off down the hall. I rushed out of the office and down to the parking lot, taking the stairwell so that I didn't have to be in the elevator at the same time with anyone for fear I couldn't hold back the flood of tears that I felt coming on. There was no way I would be able to look at anyone. I ran across the parking lot to my car, quickly unlocked the door, and climbed in.

I slammed my door shut, threw my purse into the passenger seat and buried my face in my hands and let it all out. The final nail had been hammered in. I wasn't pregnant. I had slept with my best friend at first in hopes of becoming a mother, and it had been all for nothing. Instead, I had fallen in love with him and couldn't even tell him. I didn't even have him to hold me through all this heartache, because that was what it was, pure and total heartache. I felt as if a part of me had died and that no amount of time would fix me.

I had taken my time after my appointment to drive back to the office. It was now a little after seven, and I sat in my office with my door closed. I had struggled my way through the last appointment of the day that had been waiting for me when I had gotten back. My work day was over and now I sat with a hot cup of chamomile tea trying hard to concentrate enough to be able to go over the client file for my appointment tomorrow morning. All I really wanted was to go home and curl up in bed, put the heating pad on, and zone out in front of the TV.

I looked to my cell phone that sat on the corner of my

desk, the little blinking red light reminding me that I still hadn't contacted Chase after I received the news. I really didn't have any desire to talk to him or anyone. I reached for a scrap piece of paper to make a quick note when I heard a loud, deep voice out in the hall. As the voice crept closer and my anxiety built, I was about to get up and see what was going on when my door opened and Chase strode in, Marie following behind him.

"Sir, I can't let you interrupt her...I told you, she asked for privacy. I'm sorry, Sophie, he came barging in and wouldn't stop, even after I told him you weren't taking any more clients tonight. I didn't mean to have him interrupt you. I know you said you wanted not to be bothered."

I looked into Chase's blue eyes and instantly felt a fire deep in the pit of my stomach. I glanced to Marie who stood there ringing her hands. "It's fine, Marie." I smiled weakly. I met his blue eyes again and sat back down behind my desk. Marie nodded and pulled the door closed behind her, leaving us alone.

"What the hell? Is she your own private security or something?" Chase chuckled.

"Chase, I had asked not to be bothered. She was simply doing her job," I bit out, closing the file on my desk and shutting down my laptop, then shoving both into the bag that sat at my feet.

"Do you have a minute?"

"Not really. I need to get home and get this work completed. I have an early morning tomorrow, and I am really very unprepared for it." I grabbed my coat and threw it around my shoulders.

"Listen, just give me a minute. I sent you a message today, and you didn't respond, but I've been thinking. I want to be a part of this pregnancy. I want to help you in whatever way you need. I know I said I didn't, but I do. I want to help you decorate the nursery, buy supplies, change diapers, and have my allotment of baby time."

I looked into his blue eyes, which were now filled with so much hope, want, and excitement that I didn't know what to say. It was enough that I was crushed, but now to have to face that crushing look in his eyes, an indescribable feeling came over me. I had no words. Nothing I could say would make it less painful, so instead I just stood there staring back at him.

"I want to be there for the next doctor appointment, for all the appointments, especially the ultrasound. I want to be there to hear the baby's heartbeat for the first time. I just need you to tell me when and where to be, and I'll make it happen. I want to be there for all the firsts. I want to be there for you when you deliver, when you go home. I want to be there to see his or her first steps." He pulled his phone from his pocket and flipped until he found what he was looking for. "First, we will start with the next appointment. Tell me when and where." When I didn't say anything to that, he looked up and met my eyes.

"Why the sad face? I thought you would be happy to have some sort of support system. Some help..."

I let out a sigh. "I would be grateful for the support system, but it doesn't matter, Chase." Those were the only words I could get out. I swallowed hard, continuing to pack my bag so that I could avoid what I knew was coming, what I knew had to come. I had to tell him, but honestly, I didn't even know how.

"Sure it does. Why would you say that?" He set his phone on the desk and approached me. He placed his hands on my arms, stopping me from what I was doing. He placed his finger under my chin and raised my head so he could look into my eyes.

The longer he looked into my eyes, the more my eyes burned, and I tried so hard to muster up the courage not to cry, but as soon as I blinked, a tear slipped from the corner, giving me away. "It doesn't matter, because there isn't a baby. It didn't work. I'm not pregnant."

I could see the stunned look in Chase's eyes, and then I slowly felt his hands slip down my arms as the words hit him full force. "But...that's impossible."

"But nothing. It's not impossible. There is no baby. So you're off the hook. You don't need to pretend to want to be here for me, Chase. You don't need a baby. You're a hot, single guy with your life in front of you. My little experiment, all the planning, didn't work, so things will go back to the way they were. You can go back to dating all those gorgeous women, and I will go back to my boring old life of lonely weekends, taxes, and the occasional shitty date. Thank you for trying. I've got to go though."

I turned away from his stare, zipped my bag closed, picked up my purse, and left my office, leaving Chase standing there against my desk. There was nothing more to say. I didn't look back. I couldn't. I didn't want to see the joy of him being off the hook, and I didn't want him to know any more than he already did that I was completely crushed.

I took my time walking down the hall and into the lobby where Marie sat. I approached her desk and stopped to hand her a few important documents. "Can you please make sure these get faxed tonight before you leave, and just so you know, Chase is still in my office. He is welcome to stay as long as he needs. Just let him have some time okay."

"Sure thing, Sophie. Have a good night, and I will see you tomorrow."

"You as well."

I drove slowly on my way home, a drive that would normally take me ten minutes taking me twenty. I had never been so happy to walk into the quietness of my condo. Not caring, I left a trail of my belongings all over the floor and grabbed a bottle of water from the fridge.

My heart had been heavy and my head hurt, and now I felt worse because I had walked out on Chase, but I hadn't had a choice. I didn't even know how to handle what I was feeling. I took my water, shut off the light, and made my way to my bedroom.

I shut my bedroom door, turned on the heated mattress pad so it could warm up, and put the TV on. I washed my face, tied my hair back into a messy ponytail, and changed into my favorite flannel pajama pants and T-shirt. I pulled the large blinds across the floor-to-ceiling windows, something I never did, and pulled the duvet down and crawled into bed. I fell into the large pile of pillows and pulled an extra one into my body. As I inhaled, all I could smell was Chase. The longer I lay there inhaling his scent, the longer I had to hold onto the sob that was threatening to escape my throat.

When my chest felt like it was going to explode, I finally succumbed, and a loud sob escaped me, echoing through the room. I held onto that pillow, inhaling his scent, and cried, wishing that Chase's arms were wrapped around me, trying to comfort me. I not only cried for the loss of something that could have been but for the loss of Chase as well, because no matter what, I couldn't have him as a lover or a friend. That was when the full realization hit me. I had lost both him and a baby this afternoon.

Chapter Twenty

Chase

I drove around the city aimlessly for three hours, after I had left the quietness of Sophie's office. I'd waited at least a half hour after she had left before I got behind the wheel of my car. I was now down at the waterfront.

I shut the engine off and began walking through the park back to the spot where Sophie and I had shared our second first kiss only a few weeks earlier. I sat down on an empty bench and looked out over the water. Memories flashed through my mind. I smiled at the memory of the look on her face as our lips had parted the first time.

My phone vibrated in my pocket, pulling me out of my memories. I checked my messages to see that my brothers were waiting for me at our normal restaurant location. I was about to message them to let them know I wasn't coming but decided getting out with them would do me good. I needed to pull myself out of this funk.

Twenty minutes later, I pulled into the parking lot of Wings and Things. I immediately saw that all of my brothers' vehicles were parked. I cut the engine and checked my phone once again for any message from Sophie. I was hoping for anything, a hello, fuck you, die bastard die, whatever she wanted to send, but there was nothing.

I removed my seatbelt and shoved my phone back into my jacket pocket. Walking into the restaurant I was greeted with an onslaught of waving women, most of whom I had slept with at one time or another over the years. We apparently needed to change up our location, I thought to myself, but I was polite, greeted them, even making small talk with some. I approached the bar, ordered a beer, and made my way back to where my brothers were waiting.

I slid into the booth beside Hunter and shoved my face into the menu that sat waiting for me. Carly dropped a beer in front of me, flashing me one of her smiles. When I didn't make eye contact and only mumbled a thank you, she walked away with a look of disappointment.

"What the fuck is up with you?" Bryce questioned, looking between Carter and Hunter.

"Nothing?"

"Nothing? What the fuck? Four months ago you and Carly were all over one another. You'd take her home, screw her brains out, and now you barely acknowledge her?" Bryce seemed a little pissed off and picked up his beer and took a swig.

"Mom would be so disappointed with you," Hunter said facetiously, trying to get under my skin. I knew he was doing it on purpose, since he was the only one who I'd really confided in, yet he still didn't know the outcome.

I did my best to ignore them, letting them carry on with whatever conversation they had been in the middle of before I'd arrived. I wasn't really all that hungry, and I finally shut the menu, downed the remainder of my beer, and was well into my second one before I heard my name mentioned.

I looked to Carter who sat there staring at me. "You sure you're all right?"

I nodded, downed the remainder of my second beer, and signaled for another one.

"Jesus, you should slow down there, bro. You have a car to drive home," Carter said, nodding towards the empty beer bottle.

Hunter turned to look at me. "Did you finally hear anything?"

I nodded. For the past couple of weeks, I had let my brothers believe that everything was back to normal with me and that I was back to my old dating ways. I had made up dates with numerous women to avoid our nights out. I'd made up stories of the girls I had taken home, but the truth was that, since I had left Sophie's apartment that Monday morning a few weeks ago, I hadn't been able to look at another woman, because the only one that was on my mind was Sophie. I'd spent my nights at home, watching movies, texting or chatting with Sophie on the phone, even spending one more night in her bed, but now I feared my lies were about to surface, because telling them all one thing via text was different than sitting in front of them.

"Well? Is she pregnant? Did you fulfill her need? Did your super sperm win?" Hunter and Carter chuckled at Bryce's insinuation. I, on the other hand, did not.

"When is the big day? With any luck, Mia will be expecting at the same time," Bryce said.

"What big day?" I asked, picking at the label on my beer.

"Really, Chase? You have to ask? When is the due date?"

I let out a deep breath, continuing to pick at the already mangled label on my beer bottle. I could feel them watching me as I sat there trying to decide to tell them. "All right, let me level with you guys. There is no baby. She isn't pregnant, and honestly, I'm devastated."

The silence at the table was deafening. I watched them as they looked between one another, not really sure what they should or could say. "Don't you guys have anything to say at all?" I asked.

"Why are you so devastated? I mean, you made her sign the contract, remember?" Hunter said quietly.

"I remember," I said, flinching at the memory.

"We're a little lost here, Chase," Bryce said, setting his bottle down and looking at the others. "You wanted nothing to do with everything after the deed was done. Your words, bro."

"Look, I haven't exactly been truthful with you guys." I looked to my three brothers. "I haven't been with a woman since Sophie. There have been no dates. I've been hanging out at home watching TV, playing video games, and talking or texting with Sophie. So when I've told you I couldn't do something because I had a date, I was lying."

The three of them exchanged a knowing glance, then looked back at me. "So, you want her because of the baby?" Hunter questioned.

"No. I want her no matter what. I can't get her out of my fucking mind. She's everything. Everything about her is fucking amazing."

There was the truth. It had finally moved past my lips and was now out in the open. I felt a ton of weight lifted from my shoulders for finally speaking the actual truth. I'd had a taste of her, and I didn't want to be without her, regardless of a baby. I wanted Sophie.

"Have you told her?" Carter questioned.

I shook my head. "Look, I saw the look in her eyes, that look of disappointment. I saw the look, and I know what that look means. She wants nothing more to do with me."

"Yeah, well, you don't know that until you tell her how you feel. Give her a chance to respond to your feelings."

All through dinner, I listened to each of my brothers do their best to convince me that I should talk with her and share my feelings. I also came up with every single excuse that I could think of as to why this was a very bad idea. Although, no matter what my excuses, they combated them with a reason why I was just being a coward. At the end of the night, accepting what I'd been telling myself, I'd come to the conclusion that there was no way I could tell her. I sat in the parking lot and watched as each of my brothers left.

I sat in my car, alone, rethinking each of their advice while I waited for the engine to warm, my mind constantly racing back to her face this afternoon as she stood there telling me that there was no baby. I looked at the clock; it was close to midnight. I knew she would still be up. At least I hoped she would be as I put my car into drive and pulled out of the parking lot. My brothers were right; I would regret not telling her how I felt for the rest of my life, and living with that would be harder than coming clean and telling her how I felt.

I drove through the city thinking of what I was going to say to her when I finally saw her. Should I just swoop in, grab her in my arms, kiss her, and confess everything? I stood in the elevator of her building tapping my foot impatiently as I was lifted to her floor. I ran down the hall and stopped outside of her door, then I inhaled deeply and banged on it. I wasn't going to give her the chance not to answer. I banged again, and finally the door was abruptly opened and a red-nosed, tear-stained face stood before me.

"Chase? What on earth?"

I pushed my way into her apartment, grabbing her and pulling her into me. "You, you're what I want." I pressed my lips to hers and pulled away. "Marry me?"

"Chase." She pushed her hands on my chest, trying to push me away. "Let me go."

"Not until you promise me you'll marry me."

"Let go of me!" she barked, finally pushing me hard enough that I stumbled. "You've been drinking! I don't want you to only want me when you are drunk. I want you to want me sober."

"I've had a couple beers, but I'm not drunk."

"You are. I can taste it on you."

"Sophie, I'm not. Fuck, I love you." Sure, I'd probably had too much to drink. I probably shouldn't have driven, and this was far from my smoothest performance to date, but what I was saying was the truth. It was how I felt.

"I can't do this, Chase. Please." Her hand covered her mouth and a tear escaped her eye. "Please, just go."

She turned away from me, and her shoulders started to shake. I reached out to her to pull her into my arms to comfort her, but she was too quick and stepped out of my reach. I wanted her. I wanted her so damn bad, and I stepped forward and placed my hand on her arm, but she ripped herself away from me.

"I told you to go."

I didn't say anything. I just stood there looking at her. Looking at the curves I wished to touch, the hair I longed to run my fingers through, and the body I wished to hold and worship while she lay beneath me. I had committed those feelings to memory. I'd committed those memories to mine. There was no winning. She wasn't going to change her mind, so, without a word, I walked out of her condo, shutting the door behind me. Behind us.

Chapter Twenty-One

Sophie - 5 months later

It was cold and blustery out. I glanced out my office window to see the mess of snow falling. I dug into my dish of Moo Shu Pork that Jenna had so kindly brought to me. She sat across from me rooting through her purse for her dental floss, finally finding the little blue container.

"I should have had you bring me two of these—one for now and one for tomorrow night." I giggled.

"I have no problem doing this again tomorrow night. I'll even grab two of those to-die-for cinnamon rolls from Aroma Mocha," Sophie said as she shoved the remainder of her egg roll in her mouth.

"Well that sounds like a date that I'm not going to pass up!"

"Have you heard from..."

I was about to hold my hand up to stop her from asking when Carol popped her head into my office.

"You lovelies have any hot plans for tonight?"

"Hey, Carol!" Jenna said, waving, a big smile on her face. "How are you doing?"

"I'm well, Jenna. It's so nice to see you. Please tell me that you are trying to get this girl out of here for Valentine's Day?" she said, nodding towards me.

"Well, yes, she doesn't know it yet, but I have a date lined up for her. It's getting Miss Stubborn to agree to at least meet us at the restaurant," Jenna said, pointing at me.

"Listen, the both of you. For you it may be Valentine's Day, but for me it's Singles Awareness Day. I plan to work until seven, maybe eight, then head home and have a love affair with a bottle of wine and a pizza. Perhaps a chocolate cupcake."

They both let out a loud laugh, but I was serious. I spent most of my days at the office, including the weekends. I had stopped going out for our monthly get-together. As a matter of fact, I had stopped going anywhere and everywhere that I could possibly run into Chase. I still went to Saturday-morning yoga, but afterward we either went to my place or Jenna's for coffee.

"I'll do my best, Carol, but she is a tough one."

"That she is."

"Would the two of you please stop talking about me as if I am not sitting right here."

"All right, I have to get out of here. I promised John I'd be home. He's taking me to a play. Good night, ladies."

"Night, Carol," we both shouted in unison.

I turned back to Jenna, who now sat staring at the engagement ring on her finger. Matt had finally proposed, and she was over the moon excited. I didn't blame her; they made the cutest couple, and I was so happy to see that they were finally taking the next step. I let out a loud sigh and set my fork onto the side of the container.

"Are you sure you won't join us tonight?" Jenna pleaded. "It will only be Matt and I, I swear. We miss you and really want you to join us. Plus, we are gonna talk wedding details, and you need to be there if you are going to take me up on my offer and be my maid of honor." She had invited me to join them for dinner, but I really didn't want to feel like a third wheel.

I nodded. "I'm sure. Did you see that waiting room full of people out there? Someone must help them. Besides, it's Valentine's Day. You guys should be alone. There is plenty of time to go over wedding details."

"It's just another day, Sophie. It's fine. Matt told me when he made the reservation he had already asked for a table for three."

"Well then you will have lots of room then. Really, it's

fine. I chose to work tonight so everyone else could be home. Go enjoy yourself. Maybe we can do coffee at my place this weekend. I will cook brunch or something." I shrugged. If I knew Matt and Jenna, I knew that the table for three they were claiming to have would really be a table of four and Chase would probably be the other guest. "Seriously, I'm fine. Go."

"Sophie, it's been five months. You can't keep ignoring the outside world. How will you ever meet someone?"

"Ha, Jenna, don't even start that. I'm perfectly good with staying single, okay." I turned my attention to the file that sat on top of the pile. I didn't want to be hounded. I wanted my friend to leave me in my misery and go and be with her fiancé.

"All right then, on that note, I guess I will be going. I've taken up enough of your time."

I hugged Jenna, and as she left, I wandered down the hall and grabbed another cup of coffee and went out to call in my next client. I'd been in the meeting going over the client's tax return for twenty minutes when I heard Marie raise her voice. I did my best not to pay attention to it, but when I heard her raise her voice again, I quickly excused myself.

I opened my office door and was smacked in the face with the aroma of a freshly cooked pizza. My stomach let out a loud groan, even though I'd already eaten.

"Marie? What is going on? Who ordered pizza?" I

called as I walked around the corner to see a room full of people and Marie guarding the entrance of the hallway with her life from Chase. I stopped in my tracks at the sight.

"There she is. I told you I knew she was here. Now let me in," he bit out, trying to push his way past Marie. When she blocked him again, he stepped into the first boardroom and threw the pizza box down on the table. "It's okay, you don't want to let me in to see her. It's no problem. The meeting can be done in here as well. It doesn't need to be held in her office. Oh, and it's not a problem. I have nowhere to be, so I'll wait," he said, setting my favorite bottle of wine down beside the box and turning to hand me a dozen long-stemmed red roses.

"Chase, what are you doing?" I whispered, shocked, but took the flowers from his hand, bringing them to my nose.

"I have brought you your Valentine's Day dinner." He flipped open the pizza box, exposing a heart-shaped pizza. "Double cheese. No pepperoni. And wine because I know you love wine with your pizza."

My eyes began to burn, and within seconds, they were filled with tears that I tried hard to blink away, but they spilled over the edge of my eye and ran down my cheek. I wiped at them instantly to hide them, but it was too late. Chase had already seen.

"My God, I am always making you cry," he said, taking

a step closer, reaching out and cupping my cheek, wiping away another tear with his thumb. "I've got to work on that," he mumbled.

"Chase, people are watching," I whispered. I knew the door to the boardroom stood wide open and many sets of eyes were watching from the waiting room. "Let me close the door, okay," I said, trying to step around him, but he blocked me.

"So, let them watch. Let them all watch." That was all he said before he dropped to one knee and pulled from his pocket a little box. "Sophie, I can't stop thinking of you. You're actually all I think about."

"Chase, what are you doing?"

"Shhhh..."

I watched through blurry eyes as Chase cracked open the little box he held to reveal a diamond solitaire surrounded with tiny blue sapphires.

"Chase..." I mumbled through tears.

"No, you are going to listen. I want to be with you. I want to make babies with you—many, many babies. If we can't make them, then we will adopt. I even know someone who might be able to help us out with that. Even if we don't, I honestly don't care, as long as you will walk through the rest of my life by my side."

He reached behind him and pulled from his pocket an envelope. "What is that?" I asked.

"This," he said, looking to the envelope in his hand, "is

that stupid NDA and contract that I made you sign. I was very stupid to even think about bringing it to the table. Stupid and naive to think that I would have been able to be with you and not fall head over heels in love with you. I want to be with you forever, Sophie, and if I have to I will spend the rest of my life trying to prove it to you."

He ripped the envelope in half, and then those halves in half, throwing them to the ground. "It's done, it's over, they are gone," he said, smiling up at me. "Besides, they were never legal anyways. I didn't have the heart to have them notarized." He chuckled.

"You do know I have a shredder in my office, right? It might be easier." I smiled down at him.

"Well, what do you say?"

"I say you should pick yourself and that paper up off my office floor," I said, not giving away exactly how excited I was. His face dropped, and he reached for the ripped pieces and stood up. He lifted his head and met my eyes. "Now I think you should kiss me."

Chase smiled and pulled me into his arms, kissing me deeply. As soon as we parted, he took the ring and slipped it onto my finger. I looked down at my hand and back to Chase.

"I love you too," I whispered.

The people waiting in the waiting room broke out into a loud applause, some yelling words of congratulations. I had completely forgotten they were standing there behind me watching us. I buried my face into Chase's shoulder to hide my embarrassment.

"Give us a few minutes, folks," Chase called out before closing the door to the boardroom. His lips met mine as he pushed me up against the door, kissing me hard. "I say you close up shop, come home with me, and let me worship you all night long."

"I think that sounds perfect."

Chapter Twenty-Two

Chase

The second that boardroom door clicked closed, I shoved Sophie up against the wall. I kissed her deeply, but it wasn't nearly enough. I wanted to rip her clothes off and screw her right there on the boardroom table. It had always been a fantasy of mine, one I'd not fulfilled but knew that within time we would celebrate a first for both of us. I tried, but she begged me not to, insisting that she needed to get back to the clients, especially the one she had forgotten about in her office. So, reluctantly, I let her go, and I sat waiting in the lobby of her office, my cock straining against the zipper of my jeans for an hour while she dealt with the remaining people who had insisted on seeing her before we left for the night.

I had never been so happy to see the last person leave, and shortly after Sophie came walking out of her office, her briefcase in hand, and her coat flung over her arm. She gave me a sexy smile as she walked across the lobby to where I was waiting.

"It's about time," I kidded, knowing just how important her business was to her.

We stepped out into the cold night air and I took her hand in mine as we walked across the parking lot. I stopped at my car and opened the passenger door, looked behind me and saw Sophie walked towards hers. "Where are you going?" I questioned.

"To my place," she stated.

"No, you are coming with me." I walked over, guiding her back to my car.

"Okay, but I need to stop and get a few things first then."

"Like?"

"Well, I need a toothbrush, hair care products, shower products, clothes." She looked up at me innocently.

"I have an extra toothbrush, I do have a hairdryer, and I do shower, so I have products, and there is nothing that I plan on doing with you this weekend that will require a tremendous amount of clothes. I promise." I smiled.

"Chase, don't be ridiculous."

"I'm not, trust me. What I plan on doing with you over the next twenty-four to forty-eight hours does not require clothes."

She covered her mouth as she laughed and climbed into my car. I raced through the city, and twenty minutes later, her briefcase and coat were in a pile on my floor by the doorway and a trail of clothes led the way to my bedroom.

My cock ached as I sank into her tightness. Sweat poured off my body as I pounded into her. Her cries were loud and echoing through the room. I loved the sounds she made because of me. My one hand gripped her hip and the other gripped her shoulder, holding her close to me. The harder I thrusted, the deeper I went, and the louder she became. I could already feel her tightening with every thrust and knew she was on the boarder of her release. I stopped and pulled out of her. I watched as her head dropped to the mattress, breathless.

"Why...why did you stop?" she asked breathlessly.

"I want to be able to see your face as you come." I leaned over, whispering in her ear, "Roll onto your back."

When she didn't move right away, I quickly flipped her over. She let out a laugh. I pulled her closer to the edge of the bed and quickly sank back into the heat and tightness I so loved. Her moans sent chills through me as I knew I was the one causing her to make them. It only took a second to get her right back where she had been, and I stroked her clit to help her along.

She forced her head back, lifting herself off the mattress, and let go. Her cries were louder than before, and I began to worry if my neighbors were going to hear. That worry went away quickly as I felt my balls tighten and I gritted out her name, pouring myself into her.

Minutes after cleaning her up, she lay cradled in my arms, staring down at the ring that she now wore. "What are you thinking about?" I asked as I ran my fingers through her hair.

"Just the answer to that question you asked me so long ago."

"What question?"

"Why we waited?"

I looked into her eyes. There was a seriousness behind them that, in all the years that I had known her, I had never seen before. "And what is your answer?" I asked as my heart began to pump a little faster, hoping that perhaps her answer was the same as mine.

"Honestly, I think every relationship has failed me in one way or another because of one reason. You. I think that without knowing it, in some way I have been in love with you from the start. I never really knew how to express it or how to show it, and at the risk of losing our friendship, I never was brave enough to do anything about it."

I laced my fingers through hers and pulled her into

me. I had done a lot of soul searching over the last five months, and I knew that was exactly how I felt as well. "I think you might be right," I whispered as I placed my hand on her cheek and gently met her mouth, kissing her deeply.

Monday morning I walked on air as I made my way into the boardroom. Carter, Hunter, and Bryce all sat in their usual spots, a coffee in front of them, going over whatever documents were being brought to the table. I sauntered in, dropping my suit jacket on the chair behind me, and sat down.

"Jesus, it's about time you got here," Carter complained, glancing at his watch.

"We weren't sure if we should start without you or send out reinforcements to find you," Bryce stated.

"However, we guessed we should just start without you, since we figured you were probably balls deep in your fiancée this morning." Hunter grinned.

These fuckers, I thought to myself, and I hung my head low and sat in my usual spot. I hadn't bothered to call any of them after telling them what my plan had been, so none of them knew how it had gone. I let out a breath.

"She said no. No, I don't want to talk about it, so let's get down to business," I stated with no emotion.

I almost burst out laughing at the looks on their faces as they quickly averted their eyes from me and to one another, and suddenly the mood in the room shifted.

"Jesus, man, I am so sorry," they all said in unison.

The room went quiet as I opened up the file that sat in front of my spot. I fought off the urge to smile.

"Did she give you a reason?" Hunter questioned.

I shook my head. I knew if I looked up at any one of my brothers, I would burst out laughing.

"She can't just say no without a reason," Bryce stated.

"Sure she can. Why can't she?" Carter questioned.

"Fuck that. If it were me, I'd demand an answer. Look at him. The poor ass has been through enough. He at least deserves an answer. Get her on the phone. Let's break her true Malone style."

Pretty soon, even Hunter was involved in the conversation, and my three brothers soon forgot I was sitting there. They spent ten minutes arguing amongst themselves about my problems, before I cleared my throat to remind them that I was still there and that I could hear everything they were saying.

"Hey, we're sorry, man. Totally inappropriate behavior," Carter said, shaking his head.

I chuckled to myself. "It's all good. She said yes."

"You ass." Bryce smiled. "Congrats, brother."

"So, when is the big date? You know the girls will want to know right away."

"We haven't set one yet but will soon."

"Better get to it, because as soon as we tell Mia, Autumn, and Hope, you know they are going to want to start planning everything," Bryce said, pulling me in for a hug. "Congrats, bro."

Our weekly Monday-morning meeting quickly turned into a celebratory one, which turned into a celebratory lunch.

Chapter Twenty-Three

Sophie

Chase and I had spent the better part of the week at his place discussing at great length how we were going to move forward. We had decided that I would sell my condo and move into his, which was bigger, and ultimately had the best view of not only the city but of the harbor as well. Hunter had recommended their realtor, and I found myself running through my condo a week later, cleaning like a mad woman for an appointment with her Sunday morning.

I'd just gotten out of the shower and was sitting in the living room with the paper and a hot cup of coffee in hand while waiting for her to arrive. I was reading through an article when my cell phone vibrated on the table. I glanced at my phone and laughed when I saw Jenna's name. Her message of "are you okay" caused me to giggle, and I glanced to the sparkling diamond that I now wore on my left hand. I quickly began typing a message but stopped and called her instead.

"Hello," she sang into the phone. "It's about time you called. I was beginning to wonder if this past Valentine's Day didn't do you in."

"I know. I'm sorry."

"Don't be sorry. Just tell me if you are okay."

"Listen, do you think you could meet me in a little bit?" I asked, using the same depressed voice I'd been using for the past five months, even though I was so far from that state of mind I now had whiplash.

"Of course, I can meet you. Just say where and when and I will be there. Is everything okay?" I heard her whisper something to Matt. It didn't surprise me as much as it bothered me that I had been their topic of discussion lately.

"Um, how about four at Aroma Mocha? The cafe should be pretty quiet by then."

"Oh, Sophie, at four? Come on, you need to start getting out again with humans."

"I know, I know, and I do get out with humans. I do still work, you know. Come on, please," I begged.

"Fine. I will see you at four, but only if you promise to come out with us on Friday night."

"I won't promise, but I will try, okay," I lied. I already knew we were meeting them Friday night. Chase just hadn't said anything to Matt yet.

"All right, I'll take that answer, since it's better than the last few I've been given. I'll see you in a little bit."

We both hung up the phone. Just as I set my phone down, the realtor knocked on the door.

Two hours later, I shut the door to my condo and called Chase. "All the paperwork is signed," I sang into the phone.

"Awesome. Everything go okay?"

"Yep. I'll be over in a little bit, okay? Jenna wants to have a coffee. See you tonight?"

"You know it. I'll come to your place that way we can bring some of your things here tomorrow. Sound good?"

"Sounds great. See you soon."

I slipped my cell into my purse and left my condo. I walked down to Aroma Mocha. It was a beautiful, sunny day, and I couldn't wait to share the news with Jenna. I felt like I'd been holding this secret long enough. I walked in and placed our order—coffee and muffins as always— and took a seat over in the back corner.

I'd been waiting for ten minutes when I finally saw Jenna pull the door open and walk in. She looked around the fairly empty diner and finally saw me. I had to keep my head down to contain the smile that I had hidden on my face.

"Sophie, look at you. You're an utter mess," she bit out as she slid into the seat across from me. It was true. After the realtor left, I had thrown my hair up in a messy pony-tail and put on an old T-shirt and jeans. If I was going to be packing later, I didn't want to wear good clothes.

I shrugged. "I guess, but I didn't think I looked that bad," I mumbled.

"Honey. You can't keep doing this to yourself. You can't keep hiding in your condo. We all miss you, and we are all very worried about you. I figured that after last weekend you would be good to go, but you've now been avoiding me. You didn't show up for yoga on Saturday either."

Shit, I had forgotten all about yoga, and I had promised Jenna I would be there too. I was about to explain when our coffee and muffins were placed down in front of us, and as Jenna thanked the waitress, I pulled my hand from below the table and grabbed my coffee mug.

As the waitress walked away from our table, Jenna turned towards me and was just about to say something else that would either be in the form of yelling and giving me shit or trying to comfort me, when her eyes spotted the ring I wore.

"What on earth..."

"He asked me to marry him. Obviously, I said yes," I said, wiggling my fingers.

Jenna reached for my hand, gripping it tightly and pulling it towards her.

"My God, girl, that is gorgeous," she said as she continued looking it over. Then she raised her eyes to mine and smiled. "Are you happy?"

"Jenna, seriously, I couldn't be happier. He's everything to me. I mean, there aren't many people who can say they are lucky enough to marry their best friend."

"My God, I have to call Matt," Jenna said, rifling through her purse for her cell phone. "We need to celebrate."

"Hold up. I know Chase wanted to tell Matt, so don't ruin it for him." I giggled.

"Okay, fine." Jenna pouted, putting her purse down.

"We have lots to talk about. I need a dress, and you need a dress," I said.

"We get to shop together for our wedding dresses," we sang in unison.

I could feel the excitement building, and before I knew it, we had been sitting in the coffee shop for over three hours. We had gotten lost in plans and locations and flower choices and honeymoon spots.

"This is going to be so amazing. I seriously cannot wait," Jenna said, laughing.

Suddenly, I felt a hand on my shoulder and looked up

to see Chase standing beside me, and Matt trailing behind with a tray of coffees. We had been so wrapped up that we hadn't noticed the time.

"Congratulations, guys!" Matt said, setting the tray down on the edge of the table and passing each of us our coffees.

Chase slid in beside me, putting his arm around me and pulling me into him. "I was getting worried. I called Matt to see if you were over there, and he was the one who led us here." He leaned in and kissed me.

"Sorry about that. We got caught up in wedding plans," I said, kissing him.

"And so, it starts!" Matt laughed.

"We were both afraid of that." Chase chuckled, fist bumping Matt.

We spent the better part of the night talking, laughing, and throwing around ideas. It had been one of the best days the four of us had shared together, and only the beginning of many more to come.

Chapter Twenty-Four

Chase - One Year Later

I stood at the altar with my brothers and Matt. The girls had already come down the aisle and had taken their places across from us. The doors opened at the back of the church, and the second I set my eyes on Sophie, I could feel the tears start to form. I swallowed back the lump in my throat and watched as Sophie walked down that aisle, leaving me weak in the knees. She looked absolutely stunning. Once she stood before me, I leaned in and kissed her cheek. I couldn't wait for her to be mine.

After the ceremony, we had partied the night away with our friends and family. It was midnight, and we had just finished sharing another dance when I pulled her into me and whispered that I thought it was a good time to get going. I watched the look in her eyes as she silently agreed with me. We said our good-byes and left the venue.

I rolled over and looked at my sleeping wife. Glancing at the clock, I saw it was only five; the sun was barely up. I slid my arm under her and pulled her against me, listening to the soft moan that escaped her lips. We were leaving for our honeymoon in six hours. Two weeks in Hawaii, just us, no distractions.

"Baby, good morning," I whispered, sucking her earlobe into my mouth.

"Morning," she mumbled sleepily and stretched.

"Are you ready for our next adventure?"

She opened her sleep-filled eyes and looked at me. "What time is it?" I could hear the panic in her voice at the thought we had slept in.

"It's only five. We have lots of time."

Sophie raised herself up onto her elbows and looked around the hotel room. "I almost forgot where we were." She mumbled, laughing, "Guess we should get up then and have some breakfast."

I grabbed her, pulling her back down. "No way, not yet. I haven't made love to my wife yet this morning," I mumbled, kissing the side of her neck and rolling her so I was on top.

"We can't be late." Sophie laughed and then sucked in her breath as I sucked her nipple into my mouth.

"Are you already making up excuses? My brothers did warn me of this you know." I chuckled. "Calm down. We won't be late, no worries. Just relax and let me work my magic."

Sophie let out a laugh as I squeezed her sides before kissing my way down her body. I loved watching my wife come undone, and make her come undone I did.

Three hours later, we walked hand in hand through the airport to our gate. We had lots of time, so as we wandered, we stopped in some of the shops along the way. We browsed around, each of us grabbing a couple of books and magazines for the beach. We grabbed a couple coffees and bagels along the way, too, since we hadn't had time for breakfast at the hotel.

We were now seated at the gate, both reading, both eating breakfast and sipping on hot coffee.

I looked up from my book and watched her. The soft smile on her lips as she read what must have been a funny part in her favorite author's newest rom-com. It was in those few moments that I realized I couldn't have been happier. I had married my best friend. Someone who had always understood me, always listened when I needed her to. I was only sad for a second when I realized that I had wasted all this time. She had been right in front of me all along. What mattered now was that we start our lives together.

"What's got you so serious?" she questioned, pulling me out of my thoughts.

"Nothing." I smiled and shoved my head back into my book. When I looked up again a few minutes later, I caught her watching me.

"What were you thinking about, Chase?" she asked.

"Just how much I love you," I answered, grabbing her hand and lacing my fingers through hers.

Her cheeks lit with color and she smiled. "I love you too."

The overhead speaker called out our flight number. We gathered our stuff, grabbed our bags, and made our way over to the boarding gate. I was beyond blessed, and I couldn't wait to start forever with Sophie.

A Note from the Author

Dear Readers,

I would like to thank you for taking the time to read *Finding Forever with You*. I hope you enjoyed Chase and Sophie's story. If you did, I would love it if you would drop me a review. Reviews are so important and really help me; plus I love to hear what my readers think.

What started as a single story with Hunter and Autumn has turned into two years of writing about these four brothers. It is going to be hard to for me to say goodbye to Hunter, Carter, Bryce and Chase. I hope you have enjoyed the journey as much as I have.

About the Author

S.L. Sterling had been an avid reader since she was a child, often found getting lost in books. Today, if she isn't writing or plotting, she can be found buried in a romance novel. S.L. Sterling lives with her husband and dogs in Northern Ontario.

Want to stay up to date with me, take a quick second and sign up for my Newsletter

Visit my
Website

Join my Reader Group
Sterling's Silver Sapphires

Titles by S.L. Sterling

Standalones

It Was Always You
On A Silent Night
Bad Company
Back to You this Christmas
Fireside Love
Holiday Wishes
All I Want for Christmas
Office Misconduct
The Greatest Gift
Into the Sunset

All American Boys Series

Saviour Boy
The Boy Under the Gazebo

The Malone Brother Series

A Kiss Beneath the Stars
In Your Arms
His to Hold
Finding Forever with You

Vegas MMA

Dagger

KB Worlds Everyday Heroes

Constraint